ALFRED HITCHCOCK'S MUSTACHE
& OTHER ESSAYS

ROGER ZOTTI

Visit our website at
www.StillwaterPress.com
for more information.

First Stillwater River Publications Edition

ISBN: 978-1-958217-38-2 *(paperback)*
ISBN: 978-1-958217-76-4 *(hardcover)*

Names: Zotti, Roger, author.
Title: Alfred Hitchcock's mustache & other essays / Roger Zotti.
Other titles: Alfred Hitchcock's mustache and other essays
Description: First Stillwater River Publications edition. | Paw-
    tucket, RI, USA : Stillwater River Publications, [2022]
Identifiers: ISBN: 978-1-958217-38-2
Subjects: LCSH: Popular culture--United States. | Hitchcock,
    Alfred, 1899-1980. | Motion pictures. | Sports. | History. |
    LCGFT: Essays.
Classification: LCC: PS3626.O88 A44 2022 | DDC: 814/.6--dc23

1 2 3 4 5 6 7 8 9 10
Written by Roger Zotti.
Cover design by Elisha Gillette.
Published by Stillwater River Publications,
Pawtucket, RI, USA.

To Maryann, Tom, Leslie, Katja, Roy, and Jake

Books have the power to change how we see ourselves and others. The choice is ours to harness that potential.

— *Amanda Gorman, poet*

As a steady diet, I must say I prefer writers of the second class who seem to me to have perfectly realized their talent, rather than the giants who dig deep and, while striking gold, also come on slag and muddy streams.

— *Alistair Cooke,* Alistair Cooke, A Biography

It's a wonderful thing to be able to go back to something that's a couple of years old, see the flaws in the fullness of time, and then have the chance to make corrections and polish it up — or in some cases throw the whole thing out and write a better version.

— *Ann Patchett,* These Precious Days

One day I will find the right words, and they will be simple.

— *Jack Kerouac*

Good writing is conspicuous by its absence. . . . It says just enough and no more. It has manners, not mannerisms. Good writing has all the right words — and not too many of them — in all the right places.

— *Patricia T. O'Conner,* Words Fail Me

CONTENTS

ALFRED HITCHCOCK'S MUSTACHE
& OTHER ESSAYS

INTRODUCTION

The essays about Hitchcock in *Alfred Hitchcock's Mustache* are my responses to several movies he has directed and to various books that have been written about him. The other writings in this book are on a variety of subjects that interest me, and though I'm tempted to say what interests me will interest you, I'm fully aware you have your own interests, and they probably differ from mine, and that's fine.

But give my interests a chance.

I have two hopes for this book. The first is that its essays entertain you, because, as T.S. Eliot once said, "entertainment enlarges the sympathies, stimulates the mind and the spirit, warms the heart, punctures the balloons of hypocrisy, greed, and sham, tickles the funny bone, and leaves us with the glow that comes when we have been well entertained."

My second hope is that the book's essays are mildly informative.

By the way, if you come across the word *all* in this tome, slap me hard: The word *all* is a hideous generalization and should be eliminated from the English language.

GEORGE KAPLAN DOESN'T EXIST

1

Because you were thinking of asking, and even if you weren't, here are my favorite moments from three Alfred Hitchcock movies. I'll begin with *Shadow of a Doubt* (1943) and the arrival of Charles Oakley, perfectly played by Joseph Cotton, in peaceful Santa Rosa, California, a place embodying America's best qualities, to stay with his sister Emma's family, the Newtons. He immediately charms and captivates them, especially his young niece Charlie (Teresa Wright).

But when Charlie discovers Uncle Charlie is fleeing from the police because he's a serial killer known as "the Merry Widow Murderer," her problems begin and her life changes.

Wright's performance is excellent, and, as Donald Spoto says in *The Dark Side of Genius: The Life of Alfred Hitchcock*, she "demonstrates in every scene a natural suppleness of understanding, so that her character's ordeal seems both shocking and inevitable."

As for Cotten's performance as Uncle Charlie, he radiates a frightening, disturbing evil, and "might be," Edward White writes in *The Twelve Lives of Alfred Hitchcock*, "Hitchcock's most diabolical creation."

Diabolical? Take the scene in the Til-Two Bar. Without raising his voice and enveloped by smoke, Uncle Charlie tells Charlie, "You think you know something, don't you? You think you're the clever little girl in an ordinary little town. You wake up every morning of your life and you know perfectly well there's nothing in the world to trouble you . . . and at night you sleep your untroubled ordinary sleep filled with peaceful stupid dreams. And I brought you nightmares." There's more. "How do you know what the world is like? Do you know that the world is a foul pigsty? Do you know if you rip the fronts off houses you'd find swine? The world is a hell."

Cotten's speech is one of the darkest and strongest about human nature in the entire Hitchcock canon, and he delivers it in terrifying fashion, never once taking his eyes off Charlie.

2

Notorious (1946) is about the romance between Alicia Huberman (Ingrid Bergman), whose father was a convicted Nazi spy, and a mysterious government agent named T. R. Devlin (Cary Grant), who's in love with Alicia. (Who wouldn't be?)

Spoto writes that "[the] movie's spy business was secondary to its main purpose which Hitchcock believed was to tell a love story [while] the intelligence activities should remain just that — a MacGuffin, entirely subordinate to the romance that Hitchcock wanted to emphasize in any case."

And that, folks, is your MacGuffin.

In the movie's last sequence, Grant's character rescues Alicia and becomes the Cary Grant viewing audiences have long admired. After all, for most of the movie he isn't very likeable: He and Paul Prescott (a suavely villainous Louis Calhern) are a pair of devious government agents who use her.

Here's Spoto again, this time from his superbly written *The Art of Alfred Hitchcock*: *Fifty Years of His Motion Pictures*: The movie's "final moments are remarkable [and] Hitchcock gives us perhaps the tenderest, truest love scene in his entire filmography. It's straight from the pages of a fairy tale — Prince Not-So-Charming Awakens Snow Beige — but it's also every romantic's fantasy to save the beloved from the jaws of death. That it is so breathtakingly compelling is a tribute to the talents and sentiments of the director, his writer, and his players. *Notorious* withstands multiple viewings; the older you get, the truer — the more astringently true — it becomes."

3

What a life 1959's *North by Northwest*'s main character Roger O. Thornhill (Cary Grant) lives! A carefree Madison Avenue advertising executive, Thornhill is dining one afternoon in a plush restaurant and is by chance mistaken for a man named George Kaplan. Then, poor fella, he's kidnapped by enemy agents led by the debonair Philip Vandamn (the perfectly cast James Mason). Vandamn's plan is to kill Thornhill, who he thinks is Kaplan, and make it look like an automobile accident — but it backfires. Thornhill escapes and for most of the movie is on the run.

To further complicate Thornhill's life, he becomes involved in a murder, falls in love with Eve Kendall (Eva Marie Saint, never better), and discovers that, to his chagrin, she's Vandamn's mistress and is spying on him for the Federal agents headed by a man called the Professor, played by Leo G. Carroll, who has appeared in more Hitchcock movies than any other actor and enjoys himself because he knows we know he's in a Hitchcock movie.

And who's George Kaplan and what's his purpose in the movie? Well, he's a decoy. Yes, a decoy the agents created to divert Vandamn from discovering who's spying on him.

Clearly, Hitchcock enjoys teasing viewers about Kaplan. For example: During a meeting of the agents, one of them points out that Thornhill was recently accused of murder and is on the run from the police. "Apparently the poor sucker got mistaken for George Kaplan," the agent says.

Another agent quickly replies, in one of the film's most memorable lines, "How could he be mistaken for Kaplan when Kaplan doesn't exist?"

Then the only woman agent in the group asks, "What are we going to do about Mr. Thornhill?" and the Professor matter-of-factly responds that nothing will be done, but "we could congratulate ourselves on a marvelous stroke of good fortune. Our non-existent George Kaplan, created to divert suspicion from our actual agent, fortuitously becomes a living decoy."

Ernest Lehman wrote the film's wonderful screenplay and deserves a large round of applause for his brilliant line about Kaplan, which has—and I'm not exaggerating— stayed with me ever since I saw *North by Northwest* when it was first released.

George Kaplan remains one of my favorite movie characters, and the bloke doesn't even exist. Imagine!

YES, HE WAS MARVELOUS

He was a no-frills man, who brought a lunch pail filled with power, guts, pride, talent, and character. And he fought everyone, anytime, anywhere. And he was great. He was Marvin Hagler. R.I.P. champ.
— *Teddy Atlas, boxing trainer,*
commentator, and author

1

Marvin Hagler believed he had three strikes against him as a professional prizefighter. "I'm black," he said. "I'm a southpaw. I'm good." He was wrong when he said he was good. Wrong because he was better than good: He was one of the greatest middleweights ever.

I'd rate him as the middleweight division's second greatest champion; Sugar Ray Robinson was first. (Imagine a prime Marvin Hagler against a prime Sugar Ray Robinson.)

Hagler hailed from Brockton, Massachusetts and died March 13, 2021. He was sixty-six.

He held the world middleweight championship from 1980 to 1987 and ducked no one. Vito Antufermo, Tommy

Hearns, Roberto Duran, John Magabi, and Sugar Ray Leonard were among his opponents. He stopped Antufermo in their second fight, Hearns in round three, and Magabi in round eleven. He decisioned Duran and lost his title to Leonard by decision, which is still argued about today.

He could do it all—box, punch, move. And what a finisher he was! Of his many skills, perhaps finishing a hurt opponent was his best.

When Hagler retired after his loss to Leonard, he had compiled a 63-3-2 (fifty-two KOs) record. Knocked out? Never. Knocked down? Once—and that was questionable.

The fighters who defeated him were Bobby Watts and Willie Monroe in 1976, and Leonard in 1987. He avenged the Monroe loss twice in 1977, scoring TKOs in the twelfth and second rounds. In 1980 he fought Watts again and scored a second round TKO.

Hagler was inducted in 1992 into the World Hall of Fame and then, in 1993, into to the International Boxing Hall of Fame.

2

Caesars Palace, Las Vegas, was the scene of Hagler's much disputed split decision loss to Leonard, who later said that "[the fight] was the closest I've ever come to death."

After the disputed loss to Leonard, Hagler made a clean break with boxing and never fought again. He left the United States and moved to Italy and was adored by the Italian people. Interestingly, he had a short career in several Italian action movies: *Indio* (1989) and *Across Red Nights* (1991).

In George Kimball's *Four Kings: Leonard, Hagler, Hearns, and Duran, and the Last Great Era of Boxing,* the author quotes the late trainer and HBO boxing commentator Emanuel Steward who said, "I run into Marvin from time to time when I'm in Europe. He seems very content to me. . . . The only dissatisfaction in his life, I'd say, is that he's still bitter about the Leonard decision. He still believes he won that fight and that they stole something from him. I doubt he'll ever get over that."

3

Hagler's first fight against Vito Antuofermo was in 1979, at Caesars Palace, Las Vegas, and ended in a disputed draw, though most observers believe Hagler won.

At the Boston Garden two years later, Hagler had his revenge. The Italian-born Antuofermo, who now lives in Howard Beach, New York, and is one of my favorite fighters, was a bloody mess when the contest was halted at the end of round four.

After Hagler retired and was living in Milan, Italy, Antuofermo said that "[he's] become more Italian than I am — and I was born there," a remark, writes George Kimball, that inspired sportswriter Michael Katz to quip, "That could be because so much of Vito's blood rubbed off on Marvin."

With time, Hagler and Antuofermo became friends, which is ecommon among retired fighters who were bitter rivals when they were actively campaigning.

After learning of Hagler's passing, Antuofermo told David Russell of the *Queens Chronicle*, "I'm very sad, really. Whenever I saw him, it brought back memories. I felt young when I saw him. When we got together, we were like best friends." Whenever Antuofermo visited Italy, "Hagler was the first I would call to get together with."

BOUNCING BACK

Don't give up on yourself. Your identity is never a done deal. It is always a work in progress.
                    —*Twyla Tharp,* **Keep It Moving**

Twyla Tharp was one of America's greatest dancers and choreographers, and her latest book is *Keep It Moving: Lessons for the Rest of Your Life* (2019). Tharp, who's in her late seventies, wrote her book because "I want to help others believe that constantly you can be evolving; that you don't have to accept the rumor that as the body ages it becomes less. It becomes different. Hopefully more. . . ."

Keep It Moving is, she added, a "self-survival book."

She began her dancing career in 1965 and currently lives in New York City. She has received many awards and honors, including two Emmys, a Tony, nineteen honorary doctorates, and the 2004 National Medal of Arts.

Tharp's most sagacious advice in her book is her belief that "[part] of grappling with your mortality is figuring out how to live with your pain — both physical and emotional — without making your pain the whole of your life."

One of the many excellent profiles in *Keep It Moving* is about the great French artist Henri Matisse, Pablo Picasso's rival. "First diagnosed with abdominal cancer in 1941," Tharp writes, "he lived until 1954, creating many works in his last years."

A comeback? Yes. But Tharp prefers calling it a "bounce back," a term "golfers use to measure their ability to forget a ruinous shot and move on. Bounce back. I like its unambiguous candor. You get knocked down, you bounce back up."

During Matisse's lifetime he "never abandoned his pledge to find joy in the world around him," Tharp writes. She quotes the artist as saying that "[my] destination is always the same, but I work out different routes to get there"; that "what I dream of is an art of balance, purity, and serenity [and] devoid of troubling matter"; and that "there are always flowers for those who want to see them."

An enviable and a great philosophy of life!

COMFORT AND GRACE

1

A nne Lamott's essays in *Traveling Mercies: Some Thoughts on Faith* (1999) are humorous, sad, honest, charmingly flippant, practical, perceptive, self-deprecating, sagacious . . .

They're like short stories. True ones.

And don't worry about the religious aspect of her book: She doesn't preach and is never sanctimonious, even though one of her best friends is a priest.

Here's an inkling how messed up Lamott's life was before she straightened it out: It was five o'clock one evening in the mid-1980s, and "I went back to the market and bought three sixteen-ounce Rainier Ales," she writes. "I bounced back to my house, Mary Lou Retton-like, sipped the first, took a Valium, smoked a joint, drank the second ale, and took another Valium."

Then she listened to some music.

Five days passed and "after drinking the last of my sixteen-ounce Rainier Ales, I began to resent anyone's attempts to control me—even my own."

Bushmills Irish Whiskey followed. By dawn Lamott had finished the whole bottle.

It took her a year before she admitted she couldn't control her drinking. Then "on July 7, 1986, I quit, and let a bunch of sober alcoholics teach me how to get sober and stay sober.

"God, they were such a pain in the ass."

2

Traveling Mercies contains a captivating "Overture" and twenty-four essays, including the heartbreaking "Barn Raising" and the hilarious "Aunties."

"Barn Raising" deals with Lamott's two friends, Sara and Adam, whose daughter was diagnosed at the age of two with cystic fibrosis. At first, Lamott writes, she had a vision of her friends' "disaster as a gigantic canvas on which had been painted an exquisitely beautiful picture. We all wanted to take up a corner or stand side by side and lift it together so that Olivia's parents didn't have to carry the whole thing themselves."

A few months later, the vision changed for Lamott. It was now the "wall of a barn, and I saw that the people who loved them could build a marvelous barn of sorts around the family."

Along with Sara and Adam's friends and family, Lamott let them "hate what was going on when they needed to" and "one of the hardest things to do [was] to stop trying to make things come out better than they were. . . . We offered no gift of comfort when there being no comfort was where they had landed."

Eight months after the child's diagnosis, Lamott writes, things were "pretty terrible for [Sara and Adam] . . . but at the time, they got a miracle," though "it wasn't the one they wanted, where God would reach down from the sky and touch their girl with a magic wand and restore her to perfect health. Maybe that will still happen—who knows? I wouldn't put anything past God, because he or she is one crafty mother. Still, they did get a miracle, one of those dusty little red-wagon miracles, and they understand this."

It was on the night of a lunar eclipse—which occurred at the end of September—when Lamott and her young son Sam, along with Olivia, her sister Ella, and their parents Sara and Adam, "all stared up into the sky for a long time, like millions of people everywhere were doing, so we got to feel united under the strange beams of light. You could tell you were in the presence of the extraordinary. . . . Olivia kept clapping her hands against the sides of her face in wonder, as if she were about to exclaim, 'Caramba!' or 'Oy!' When the moon was bright and gold again, she ran up the stairs after her sister and Sam, who were cold and had gone inside to play."

"Aunties" is set in Huatulco, Mexico, probably in the 1980s, and early one morning Lamott plans on going to the beach with her young son Sam. She intends wearing her expensive black bathing suit that she was able to put on several years ago, she says, "without bruising."

Now meet the aunties. Lamott writes: "I had decided I was going to take my thighs and butt with me proudly wherever I went. I would treat them as if they were my beloved aunties. . . . So we walked along, the three of us, the aunties, and I imagined that I could feel the aunties beaming, as if they had been held captive in a dark closet too long, like Patty Hearst. . . . It did not trouble me that parts of my body—the aunties parts—kept moving even after I had come to a full halt. Who cares? People just need to be soft and clean."

3

The most memorable passage in "Barn Raising" is when Lamott writes that "Now, seeing [Olivia] on the night of the eclipse, her upward gaze of pure child wonder, I find it both hard to remember when she wasn't sick and harder to believe she is."

In "The Aunties" Lamott's biggest strength is her belief that "there's beauty in becoming so comfortable at being a mother, and a writer; there is grace in comfortableness."

VIKINGS AND ALL THAT

A family reunion drama, *Rocket Gibraltar* (1988) hasn't received the critical and commercial recognition it deserves. Set in the Sagaponack Village of Long Island in the 1980s, the main character is the perfectly cast Burt Lancaster as the widowed and terminally ill Levi Rockwell. A blacklisted writer during the McCarthy era, he's celebrating his seventy-seventh birthday. His son, daughters, and grandchildren will arrive at his home to celebrate with him.

The movie's cast includes Sinead Cusack, Bill Pullman, Frances Conroy, Patricia Clarkson, Kevin Spacy, Macaulay Caulkin, and Suzy Amis. Amos Oz wrote the screenplay and Daniel Petrie (*Resurrection*, *A Raisin in the Sun*) directed.

In Gary Fishgall's *Against Type: The Biography of Burt Lancaster*, he quotes the actor as saying that "I immediately wanted to do [*Rocket Gibraltar*]. It was a film with some depth, with some meaning, and a lot of powerful emotions. It was the same experience as when I first read *Atlantic City*. I don't often get the really good parts nowadays because I'm long past my so-called motion picture prime in terms of the box office. So I have to wait and hope something good comes along now and then."

What to look for

It's the wonderful last scene, the one where Rockwell's grandkids give him the Viking funeral he wanted. (Keep the grandkids in mind because they're as important as Lancaster's character.)

Also, keep an eye on those fascinating moments of communication between Rockwell and Blue, his youngest grandson. Sometimes they speak to each other, but at other times they have what Kate Buford, in her biography *Burt Lancaster: An American Life*, called a "psychic rapport."

By the way, Lancaster's Rockwell loves Jackson Pollock's paintings, Billie Holiday's singing, and Fred Astaire and Rita Hayworth's dancing.

HITCHCOCK AND THE LADIES

I doff my hat to four of Alfred Hitchcock's leading ladies: Joan Fontaine, Ingrid Bergman, Alma Reville, and Tippi Hedren. I'll begin with Fontaine, who starred as the second Mrs. de Winter in *Rebecca* (1940), along with Sir Laurence Olivier as her husband, Maxim de Winter. It was Hitchcock's first American movie and winner of the year's Oscar for Best Picture.

According to Peter Ackroyd in *Alfred Hitchcock: A Brief Life*, Fontaine told Hitchcock early on during filming that "she had run out of tears" for a particular scene. Hitchcock asked her what he could do to make her continue crying, and she replied that maybe he should slap her. So he slapped her and "she began sobbing."

Maybe the slap inspired her to work with Hitchcock a year later in *Suspicion*. No, this time she wasn't slapped, but her major worry was that Hitchcock wasn't paying attention to her. She was comforted when co-star Cary Grant told her if Hitchcock was pleased with an actor's work, he wouldn't say anything to the actor.

And for her performance in *Suspicion*, Fontaine received the Oscar for Best Actress.

Years later Fontaine summed up her experiences working with Hitchcock this way: "[Hitchcock and I] liked each other, and I knew he was rooting for me," but he had "a strange way of going about it."

In 1979, Hitchcock was the recipient of the American Film Institute Life Achievement Award, but before presenting the award to him, Oscar winner Ingrid Bergman, who starred in three Hitchcock movies— *Spellbound* (1945), *Notorious* (1946), and *Under Capricorn* (1949)—called him "an adorable genius."

Then she related an incident that happened during the filming of *Spellbound*. Confused and upset because she couldn't summon the emotion required for a particular scene, she told Hitchcock about her problem. "Fake it!" was his response. (No, he didn't slap her.)

Bergman told the audience it was the best advice anyone ever gave her about acting.

Alma Reville, Hitchcock's wife, was the most important person in his life. "She acted as his battery as well as a protective layer between him and the daunting unpredictability of other people, oiling the Hitchcock machine with diplomacy and emotional intelligence," Edward White writes in *The Twelve Lives of Alfred Hitchcock*. "She worked formally or informally, in a variety of roles on Hitchcock films· development producer, assistant director, writer, casting producer, script supervisor, all-around editorial adviser."

Hitchcock wouldn't have been Hitchcock without Alma.

Tippi Hedren wasn't exaggerating when she claimed Hitchcock mistreated her during the filming of *The Birds* (1963) and *Marnie* (1964). In *The Birds,* the cruelest thing that happened to her occurred during the scene when birds attacked her character, Melanie Daniels.

Believing that they were going to be mechanical, she "arrived on the set [and] realized that the bird handlers had arrived with protective gloves and boxes of furious birds," Ackroyd writes. "She was asked to stand in a corner of the set while the handlers threw pigeons, gulls, and crows towards her." It looked like "a ritual stoning. . . . As the filming continued, she became covered in bird excrement."

There's more. Ackroyd writes that a few days later, "the birds were tied to her with elastic bands so they would perch all over her." After the scene was filmed, studio doctors ordered her to take several days off. (It wasn't "at all clear, however, that [Hitchcock] was engaged in an illicit act of hostility toward the actress.")

Hedren recovered but admitted it was "the worst week of my life."

During the filming of *Marnie* a year later, Diane Baker, who played Liz Mainwaring, told Ackroyd that "I never saw Tippi enjoying herself with the rest of the cast. . . . And [Hitchcock] demanded that every conversation between [them] be held in private."

In January of that year, Hedren was presented with the Photoplay Award for the year's most promising actress, but, Baker says, "[Hitchcock] refused her permission to fly to New York [to accept the award]. He did not want her taken out of character, which he had slowly and meticulously created for her."

But Hitchcock had his defenders, one of them being Jay Alan Presson, who wrote *Marnie*'s screenplay and claimed that "Hitch was only trying to make a star out of [Hedren]. He may have had something like a crush on her" though "there was nothing overt." Presson believed that "he would never in one million years do anything to embarrass himself. He was a very Edwardian fellow."

After Hedren's experience of being shit on and having her face pecked by a variety of beady-eyed, greedy, winged creatures in *The Birds*, I wonder why she returned to work for Hitchcock in *Marnie*.

Or is it shat on?

AND THEN THERE'S MAE WEST

1

Sportscaster and news anchor Jim Lampley, in his Foreword to Spring Toledo's book of boxing essays, *In the Cheap Seats* (2016), is correct when he says that "[you] can't do more to prepare yourself to write boxing better than Toledo has done."

Updated in 2021, Toledo's book contains thirty-four superbly written and well-informed chapters, including "Me and Mr. Jones" and "The Ringside Belle."

Turning to "Me and Mr. Jones," Toledo, one of America's foremost boxing scholars, writes about how the great Roy Jones, Jr. reacted to the February 25, 1995, middleweight fight between Nigel Benn and Gerald McClellan at the London Arena.

A three-to-one favorite, McClellan was stopped in the tenth round. "In the moments after losing the fight," according to the September 2020 *Boxing Guide*, "and walking back to his corner, McClellan collapsed. He was rushed to the Royal London hospital where he received life-saving brain surgery [and] a blood clot was removed. [Dr. John

Sutcliffe] gave Gerald a 50% chance to live but declared his boxing career over."

McClellan regained consciousness after being in a coma for two weeks, and it "wasn't until August [that he was] able to return home."

The Boxing Guru quotes McClellan's sister Lisa as saying that "Gerald is a fighter. He is resourceful . . . despite being completely blind and 80% deaf. He can feed himself but requires help with other functions. His short-term memory is getting better. His comprehension and understanding has slowly improved over the years. He is not able to walk unassisted due to [the] areas of his brain that are damaged."

When Roy Jones, Jr. was active as a fighter, he never visited McClellan, Toledo says, though "he has donated generously to the McClellan fund."

Why? Why didn't he ever visit McClellan? "Jones became haunted by what happened for years," Toledo writes, and believed that "I don't need to [visit Gerald]. It would make me quit boxing."

2

"The Ringside Belle," the book's final chapter, is about Brooklyn-born Mae West. That's right! Mae West of big screen movie fame.

"What excited her was a fellow with a cauliflower ear or a busted nose," Toledo writes. Hence her fondness for many prizefighters.

She was also attracted to shady characters like Owney Madden. Her telephone call to Madden, "a gangland murderer and bootlegger who became the underworld king of New York in the 1920s," convinced him to use his influence "to get [Joe] Louis a title shot" against James J. Braddock. As boxing fans know, on June 22, 1937, at Chicago's Comiskey Park, Louis knocked out Braddock in the eighth round to become the first African American heavyweight champion since Jack Johnson.

Step back to 1927, ten years before the Louis vs Braddock title fight. West was in the audience watching middleweight William "Gorilla" Jones fight at Madison Square Garden. At a local bar after the fight Jones saw West and her escort, Toledo writes, "and sent over a round of drinks. West liked his moxie and invited him to see her at the theater. After the show West found that she also liked his heroic musculature and invited him to her dressing room."

Toledo writes about the time, several months later, that a big mouth made a nasty remark about West outside a bar—she and Jones had become lovers by then—and the prizefighter quickly flattened the bloke.

And how did West react? She admonished Jones. "Let 'em talk," she said. "I made four million because people were saying nasty things about me and you shouldn't get into a fight to change that opinion."

Take the 1930 novel West wrote titled *Babe Gordon*. In it, Toledo writes, she "flaunted her preference for prizefighters and taboo topics such as black/white affairs and nymphomania." (She delighted in shocking respectable sensibilities because, as she once said, "Those who are easily shocked should be shocked more often.")

After West died on November 22, 1980, at age eighty-six, she was heralded by the African American press "as a friend and heroine. Headlines trumpeted her disregard of contrived color lines," Toledo writes. "Columnist Bill Lane wrote that she had 'something within her that transcended clear skin and sexy hips. She had a humaneness that broad jumped unpretentiously over whiteness and blackness.'"

DASHIELL HAMMETT AND FALLING BEAMS

1

The Flitcraft story, which is found in the chapter titled "G in the Air," is the most important and memorable aspect in Dashiell Hammett's novel *The Maltese Falcon* (1929). The scene takes place in private detective Sam Spade's Belvedere apartment, and he tells the treacherous Brigid O'Shaughnessy, his client, a story about a man named Flitcraft, who's married, the father of two boys, a homeowner, and a successful realtor. A model citizen, that Flitcraft.

Flitcraft's story begins in 1922, and the setting is Tacoma, Washington, on a September afternoon. Flitcraft is on his lunch break and passes a building under construction. Suddenly a beam falls ten stories and narrowly misses him. When it hits the sidewalk, a piece of cement chips off and cuts his neck.

"He was scared stiff, of course," Hammett writes, "but he was more shocked than really frightened." Shocked because he realized that without warning a person's life could be ended at random by a falling beam" — and that "men died at haphazard like that."

Flitcraft realizes it was as if "somebody had taken the lid off life and let him look at the works," and the realization turns his life upside down. That afternoon he leaves his family and travels to Seattle. From there he goes to San Francisco, where he lives for several years. Then he settles in Spokane, changes his name to Charles Pierce, opens a successful automobile business, remarries, fathers a son, and lives productively and comfortably.

Five years later Spade meets Mrs. Flitcraft, who tells him she knows someone who lives in Spokane and saw a man resembling her husband. She hires Spade to investigate, and he discovers the man is her husband. Because she believes what he did to her and their children years ago was "silly" and a "trick," she wants nothing to do with his reappearance.

2

In Sally Cline's biography of Hammett, *Dashiell Hammett: Mystery Man*, she questions if "Hammett appreciate[d] the irony that his most famous and meaningful passage" — the Flitcraft story — "which gave *The Maltese Falcon* its point and stood as a symbol for all his work was entirely left out of this iconic film directed by John Huston?"

I hold Hammett knew irony was an integral part of existence, and the Flitcraft story not being included in Huston's movie was, well, simply an example of life's irony.

And speaking of irony, while Flitcraft was living happily as Charles Pierce in Spokane, Spade says to O'Shaughnessy that "I don't think he even knew he had settled back naturally into the same groove he had jumped out of in Tacoma."

I think Spade is wrong. He underestimated Flitcraft's

intelligence and ability to adjust, and that after Flitcraft became Charles Pierce, he relished living a comfortable life in Spokane similar to the life he had lived in Tacoma five years ago.

What he did, as Hammett writes in the novel's two most shrewdest sentences, was adapt "himself to beams falling. And then no more of them fell, and he adjusted himself to them not falling."

(That's the part Spade likes best about the entire Flitcraft story, and so do I.)

TENNIS, ANYONE?

1

One of Hitchcock's best and most suspenseful movies is 1951's *Strangers on a Train,* starring Farley Granger as popular tennis star Guy Haines and Robert Walker as flamboyant wacko Bruno Anthony.

Pay close attention to the opening sequence because it sets the film's action in motion. The location is Union Station, Washington, D.C., in the 1950s. A taxi stops and a well-dressed young man emerges. Then a second cab appears and another man exits.

The Hitchcock touch is evident as his camera follows the shoes of both men as they enter the train's lounge car and sit across from each other.

And in what seems to be sheer chance, but really isn't, Guy's right shoe bumps Bruno's right shoe, which leads to a conversation between them. Before long the baby-faced Bruno, who's aware of Guy's intention to divorce his wife Miriam (Laura Elliott), tells him about an idea he has been contemplating.

Bruno: It's so simple, though. Two fellows meet accidentally, like you and me. Each one has somebody he'd like to get rid of. No connection between them at all. Never saw each other before. So, they swap murders.

Guy: Swap murders? [Laughs]

Bruno: Each fellow does the other fellow's murder, then there's nothing to connect them. Each one has murdered a total stranger. Like, you do my murder. I do yours.

Guy: Coming to my station.

Bruno: For example, your wife, my father. Crisscross.

Guy: What?

Bruno: We do talk the same language, don't we?

My take on Guy and Bruno's meeting aboard the train is that Bruno planned it in advance, and that chance, a common theme in many of Hitchcock's films, has nothing to do with their bumping shoes and what follows. A cunning bastard, Bruno knew which train Guy had boarded, deliberately sat across from him, and knowingly placed his foot so that Guy would bump it, thus beginning one of the screen's most bizarre relationships.

What to look for

Along with the crucial scene when Guy first meets Bruno on the train, less obvious but just as important is when Guy learns his wife Miriam won't give him a divorce. He telephones Ann Morton (Ruth Roman), the woman he's leaving Miriam for, and, enraged, tells her he'd like to break Miriam's neck.

Though Guy thinks about murdering Miriam, it's Bruno who does the deed. But isn't Guy almost as guilty as Bruno because, after all, in the world according to Alfred Hitchcock, no one is innocent?

3

A word about Hitchcock's villains, most of whom don't look like villains: Always well dressed and soft-spoken, Bruno Antony of *Strangers on a Train* is a pleasant looking, charming young man, though of course, as we know, he's dangerously looney. In *Vertigo*, Tom Helmore's wealthy Gavin Elster is the personification of suavity and self-possession who, when the movie is over, has gotten away with murder and is most likely living an untroubled life in Southern France. In *Shadow of a Doubt,* Joseph Cotten's Uncle Charlie is handsome and amiable, until we learn the murderous truth about his past; Anthony Perkins' Norman Bates of *Psycho* is an all-American boyish looking young man who wouldn't hurt a fly until, that is, he begins talking about his mother. In sophistication and detachment, the twin of Tom Helmore's Gavin Elster, is the dignified and dangerous James Mason's Philip Vandamn of *North by Northwest*. William DeVane's Arthur Adamson of *Family Plot*, with his perfect hair, precise and annoying phrasing, and immaculate tailor-made suits, is a cold-blooded thief and killer. Who can forget Leo G. Carroll's devious, soft spoken, and very intelligent Dr. Murchison, the murderer in *Spellbound*?

I'll state the obvious because it's obvious: What most of Hitchcock's murderers have in common is their ability to charm the people with whom they come into contact because, well, they don't look different from you and me.

SOLDIER, SENATOR, MOTHER

When the only obstacle is effort, then there is no obstacle, because I will move Heaven and Earth to get what I want, even if I have to do it one pebble at a time.

—*Tammy Duckworth*, **Every Day Is a Gift**

1

The remarkable Illinois Senator Tammy Duckworth praises Harry Reasoner's 1971 ABC News commentary about helicopter pilots in her memoir *Every Day Is a Gift* because, she writes, "it captures essential truths about how [helicopter pilots] are different from other pilots."

Reasoner begins: "The thing is, helicopters are different from planes. An airplane by its nature wants to fly, and if not interfered with too strongly by unnatural events or by a deliberately incompetent pilot, it will fly. A helicopter does not want to fly. It is maintained in the air by a variety of forces and controls working in opposition to each other, and if there is any disturbance in this delicate balance, the helicopter stops flying, immediately and disastrously.

"There is no such thing as a gliding helicopter."

Reasoner concludes that "helicopter pilots are brooders, introspective anticipators of trouble. They know if something bad has not happened, it is about to."

"That 'introspective anticipators of trouble' line," Duckworth writes, "describes me to a T."

2

Duckworth is a double amputee, and her memoir is inspirational but never mawkish. It is, she writes, a "love letter to America."

Born to a Thai Chinese mother and an American marine in Bangkok, Thailand, Duckworth lived a poverty-stricken and nomadic childhood. At times, she and her family were close to homelessness. Of course, growing up as an Asian American she experienced her share of prejudice.

And she beat those obstacles! After graduating from high school, she moved to Washington, D.C., and graduated from George Washington University. Then she joined the Army Reserves where she learned to fly helicopters.

3

For Duckworth, thirty-six years old at the time, November 12, 2004, was, she writes, "the day the world exploded." She was flying a Blackhawk helicopter in Iraq when a "rocket propelled grenade blew through the plexiglass bubble at my feet and detonated in a violent fireball right in my lap. The explosion vaporized my right leg. It blew my left leg up into the bottom of the instrument panel, shearing off the shin below the knee and leaving my lower leg hanging by just a thin thread of flesh. . . . In a single, shattering instant, my body was blown apart. My skin was burned and riddled with shrapnel, and blood began pumping out of my wound.

"In addition to the traumatic injuries to my lower extremities, the bones of my right arm were shattered, the skin and muscle pulverized. There was no pulse in my right hand, which was pale and lifeless."

Duckworth spent thirteen months at Walter Reed recovering from her injuries and learning to walk on prosthetic legs.

4

It's easy to become appalled when you learn what Duckworth encountered in her 2006 campaign for retiring Republican Henry Hyde's House of Representatives seat. "Desperate not to lose Henry Hyde's seat," she writes, "the Republicans threw everything they had at me during the campaign, including spending thousands of dollars on blatantly racist ads that darkened my skin, widened my already moon-shaped face, and turned my eyes into slits."

She lost the election, a big reason being because she isn't white and old and male.

In 2008, President Barack Obama offered her "the position of Assistant Secretary for Public and Intergovernmental Affairs at the United States Department of Veterans Affairs" — which she accepted.

In 2012, age forty-four, Duckworth was elected to the House of Representatives. Her opponent was the Tea Party's Joe Walsh, and one of his tactics — which didn't work — was to criticize her for, he said, "speaking about [her military experience] publicly. I'm running against a woman who, by God, it's all she talks about. Our true heroes, the men and women who serve us—it's the last thing in the world they talk about."

Duckworth retaliated on MSNBC: "My military experience was the core of my life—was I really supposed not to talk about it? The simple truth was, being an injured female soldier helped me bring attention to the causes I cared about. If I could use it as a platform to do good, I had absolutely no qualms about it."

She beat Walsh by over twenty thousand votes.

Duckworth, who retired from military service in 2014, ran for the Illinois senate in 2016 and defeated Republican incumbent Mark Kirk. She became the first Thai American woman born in Thailand elected to Congress, the first female double-amputee in the Senate, and the first Senator to give birth while holding office.

SHE'S ON EVERYBODY'S MIND

1

Quietly patriotic but without the arrogance and ignorance that passes for patriotism today is the best way to describe director Arthur Penn and Oscar-winning screenwriter Steve Tesich's *Four Friends* (1981).

Set in East Chicago, Indiana, during the troubled and creative 1960s, the movie follows Danilo (Craig Wasson), David (Michael Huddleston), Tom (Jim Metzler), and free-spirited Georgia (Jody Thelen) from high school to their late twenties. The three young men are in love with Georgia, who believes she's the reincarnation of the great dancer Isadora Duncan. Like Duncan, Georgia lives on the edge of things.

One of the movie's key scenes is between Georgia and Danilo and proves Roger Ebert's contention, in his review of *Four Friends*, that "they have grown up, some."

> **Georgia:** I wanted to love all three of you. [Pause] Just you. Just you. Just you. Oh Christ! Just you. You.
> **Danilo:** Me? Ha!
> **Georgia:** It's not funny.

Danilo: You want to know the truth? I wish I had two lives to live. I'd like to live one of them without you.

Georgia: [Crying] You're not the only one.

Danilo: [Pause] Well, we're not making peace, are we?

Georgia: [Crying] Peace? Never! [They embrace] Why does everything take so long?

Georgia's delivery of the final line is a mix of grief, anger, and hope, and the highlight of Thelen's outstanding performance.

The movie's other crucial scene is the last one. The four friends are together on a beach with their families. It's evening. They're talking, toasting marshmallows, and laughing. They're having a joyous time because they're together again. You realize how close they are and that they'll be friends forever.

At the same time, you can't help wondering if Georgia has changed, or if she's the same Georgia she has always been.

Georgia: [Eyes ablaze with enthusiasm] Hells bells, honey. It's a big country. [Looking at Danilo] This move's yours, the next one's mine. You know what we've never done?

Danilo: A lot of things.

Georgia: You got it, kiddo.

2

Back in the day, in what seems like another lifetime, or even a dream, I taught an English composition course at a local community college and showed *Four Friends*. ("Students," I said, "your assignment is to write a 1.5- to 2-page paper about what you believe is the most important aspect of the movie and why. Be specific," and I repeated the word *specific* with more heft.)

A week later, here's what happened before class began: A young man, a good student, arrived early, walked to my desk, and mooned, "I'm in love."

> **RZ:** You're in love?
> **Young Man:** With Georgia . . .
> **RZ:** That's true for most of us who see *Four Friends*. Honest!

A moment of silence. And then we sang, or tried to sing, "Georgia on My Mind."

Georgia, Georgia
The whole day through
Just an old sweet song
Keeps Georgia on my mind
I said Georgia, Georgia
A song of you (a song of you)
Comes as sweet and clear as moonlight through
    the pines
Other arms reach out to me
Other eyes smile tenderly
Still in peaceful dreams I see
The road leads back to you . . .

We sounded pretty good and gave ourselves a well-earned round of applause. We sang—and when he finished we didn't care if Ray Charles' version was better than ours.

PAGING PRECINCT 15

SYLVIA

Sipowicz, Simone, Medavoy, Kelly, Fancy, Russell, Martinez, Lesniak, Costas, and Abandando were some of the characters on the gritty Emmy award winning police procedural *NYPD Blue* (1995-2003). Set in New York City, the ABC ensemble drama was created by Stephen Bocho and David Milch.

For the show's first six seasons, Sharon Lawrence played Assistant District Attorney Sylvia Costas. The chemistry between her character and Dennis Franz's burly veteran detective Andy Sipowicz, the show's main character, was compelling. Eventually this seemingly mismatched couple fell in love, married, and had a son.

Because of Sipowicz's drinking problems, their marriage, putting it mildly, had its ups and downs.

In Costas' final appearance, she was shot and killed while in court. Her last words to Sipowicz were, "Take care of the baby."

In an interview with Lawrence titled "The Women of *NYPD Blue*," she discusses her co-stars, including Gail O'Grady's Donna Abandando and Kim Delaney's Diane

Russell. "Gail as Donna Abandando was just a stroke of brilliance," Lawrence says. "The perfect casting for a role that could have been so much less original. She brought to it a purity which is a tough thing to do."

Abandando's style "wasn't unbelievable because in those urban areas there are women who have that style. [Gail's] perfect face, and with the outside styling of her hair and wardrobe, and [her] take on the character, was a real labor that you never expected."

As Diane Russell, Lawrence continues, "Kim really fit in with the boys. She knew how to be one of the boys, and that's not an easy thing to do. When Kim came on the show, I was very excited."

From the start her character and Bobby Simone, played by Jimmy Smits, "were a perfect fit, and they looked great together. Kim benefited more than anyone from the viewpoint of material the writers were able to do for her. They explored alcoholism and addiction."

GREG

Played by New Hampshire born, Emmy award winning Gordon Clapp, Greg Medavoy was my favorite *NYPD Blue* character.

At first his fellow detectives and the show's viewers thought he was a joke. Neuroses? It seemed he had all of them. Allergies? Name one and he had it.

Too, he had a messy domestic life involving a shrewish wife, but more important was his romance with squad room secretary Donna Abandando.

When he spoke, he often s-s-stammered, and he seemed to lack self-confidence and was easily confused. But with time he won the respect of his co-workers and the TV audience by proving he was a smart, quietly confident, brave detective concerned about his fellow detectives.

A standout scene exemplifying Medavoy's sincerity and willingness to help others occurs when he offers advice to his detective partner, the younger and troubled Baldwin Jones (Henry Simmons), who's having romantic problems with, as Medavoy knowingly tells him, "a beautiful woman you work with—I been there." Medavoy tells him that "I don't know if anyone ever told you about our former [secretary] Donna Abandando. How beautiful she was. Knockout. I mean gifted physically. And her and me, you know . . . I was going somewhere with that."

"I got what you're saying, Greg, and I appreciate it," Jones says.

"Just give it space," Medavoy adds. "You guys will be all right."

Jones appreciated Medavoy's advice because it was heartfelt, and, as Medavoy told him, *I been there.*

That's Medavoy at his best!

Say after me: The best *NYPD Blue* years were the Sipowicz/Simone episodes, especially when Medavoy was given an ample amount of camera time.

"YOU MADE THEM FEEL FREE"

1

In *The Chaperone* (2018) Elizabeth McGovern is reunited with Michael Engler, her *Downton Abbey* (2010-2015) director, and its screenwriter Julian Fellowes. Her character, Norma Carlisle, lives an unhappy domestic life in conservative Wichita, Kansas, in the 1920s. When we first meet her, she's married, the mother of twin boys, and in her mid-thirties.

One afternoon she volunteers to chaperone fifteen-year-old Louise Brooks — yes, Louise Brooks who later became a silent movie star — to New York. A rebellious, sometimes bratty, and talented young lady with a mind of her own, Brooks has been accepted at the prestigious Denishawn School of Dance and Related Arts.

2

Roger Zotti: Talk about the 1920s

Elizabeth McGovern: Well, America was changing. Women were finding themselves, their voices. They were freeing themselves from many traditions of the past. In the film, it's happening to both Brooks, played brilliantly by Haley Lu Richardson, and to my character.

RZ: How would you characterize Norma when she leaves New York near the end of the movie and returns to Wichita?

EM: When she returns it's in the 1940s. She's no longer the straightlaced Norma Carlisle of her Wichita days. In New York, she underwent a successful journey of self-discovery and became a stronger, better person. In Wichita, Norma finds Louise despondent and immediately gives her encouragement. With total honesty and conviction, she tells her, "Don't make your two German films nothing. Don't you remember every shop girl, every office worker — they all copied your look. They copied your hair. Don't you know why? You made them feel free. You changed things, Louise, you did."

When Brooks tells her she's thirty-five years old, broke, nowhere to go, and "used up," Norma replies: "Horse feathers! You don't like yourself! You don't like your parents! You don't like this town! Why come back? Are you a homing pigeon for misery? Get on a train and go. I'm certain you are not used up. I'm certain there is quite a bit of you left."

Of course, Hollywood hated Brooks and she in turn hated Hollywood. She moved back to New York in 1943 and discovered the only career that paid well for an unsuccessful actress was becoming a high-priced call girl. But that's another story for another time. Maybe Michael and Julian will tackle it.

RZ: In the movie there's that heart-wrenching scene between Norma and her biological mother—Mary O'Dell (Blythe

Danner, in a superb cameo). Mary abandoned Norma soon after she was born. Norma was raised in a Catholic orphanage in New York, and as a teenager was adopted by a Wichita family.

EM: When Norma was in New York, she learned that Mary lived in Haverhill, Massachusetts. So, she wrote her a letter and they agreed to meet in Central Park. At first the meeting is amicable, but it deteriorates when Norma learns her mother still doesn't want anything to do with her. Noticeably upset, she says to Mary, "You don't want my address, do you? You don't want to know how to get in touch with me? You don't want to meet your grandsons. "

Though it's painful for her, Norma accepts her mother's rejection. She won't tell her mother's husband and their children that their mother had a daughter when she was an unmarried teenager.

In New York, Norma falls in love with the kindest, most gentle of men, a German immigrant handyman named Joseph, wonderfully played by Geza Rohrig. Eventually, Joseph, his young daughter, and Norma return to Wichita together. There, Norma is going to introduce him to her sons, husband, and friends as her brother.

RZ: In that scene on the train—when Norma, Joseph, and his young daughter are returning to Wichita—we learn how far she has come from the Norma of Wichita she once was. We learn how realistic she is now about the world in which she lives. Her plan is for Joseph, as you said, to pose as her brother, but he tells her it's "so dishonest." It's one of the movie's most significant scenes.

EM: "In a better world we would shout who we are from the rooftops," Norma says to Joseph. "But I can't wait for a

41

better world, Joseph. I'm living now and I want to be happy. And if it doesn't work, my beloved brother, you will have to find a job and leave town with your daughter. But I think it will work because I think we want it to work." Do you remember what he says and their reaction?

RZ: Indeed, I do. He says, "If they repeal Prohibition, can I have a beer?"

EM: And then we laugh.

ALFRED HITCHCOCK'S MUSTACHE

[Hitchcock] was simultaneously the artist and the crowd-pleaser.

—*Edward White,* **The Twelve Lives of Alfred Hitchcock**

1

The magazine was called *The Mustache Manual* (1945-1977). Published twice yearly, it contained mini-biographies and photos of famous twentieth-century movie actors, directors, and producers who sported mustaches for at least two weeks. Alfred Hitchcock was included in the publication because in the nineteen-twenties—1921, to be specific—he grew a pencil thin mustache similar to the one Lew Ayres exhibited in 1946's *The Dark Mirror*, which Robert Siodmak directed.

Hitchcock had directed a 1925 silent movie titled *The Pleasure Garden*. I haven't seen it and don't recognize any of the cast, but according to *The Mustache Manual*, Virginia Valli, who played the movie's main character, would make a habit of teasing the director about what had sprouted above his upper lip.

Hitchcock admitted the more he responded to her taunts, the more she teased him. Voila! He shaved it off after the film was released. And I'm not trying to be smart-alecky, which I sometimes am, but that's all you need to know about Hitchcock's mustache because that's all I know about it.

(You have to admit that *Alfred Hitchcock's Mustache* would make a catchy title for a book of essays.)

According to the 1987 *A Guide to Alfred Hitchcock's Movies*, its author says that any essay written about Hitchcock's mustache must include a commentary about the following scene from his charming, feel good comedy *Psycho* (1960), which is when Norman Bates (Anthony Perkins) is in a jail cell attired in his mother's clothing—poor Normie suffers from some kind of identity disorder and, in his warped mind, has become his mother—and there's a fly cheerfully buzzing near him. (Where's a fly swatter when you need one?)

"They're probably watching me," he says. "Well, let them. Let them see what kind of a person I am. I'm not even going to swat that fly. I hope they are watching—they'll see. They'll see and they'll know, and they'll say '*why, she wouldn't even harm a fly!*'" Then Norman fiendishly grins at the camera . . .

That scene surprised and disturbed many viewers, but for me it ranks second, maybe even third, on my *Psycho* shock meter. And if you think my first choice is the scene when Marion Crane (Janet Leigh) is stabbed in the shower—remember those screeching violins?—or when Martin Balsam's insurance detective Milton Arbogast is stabbed on the stairs inside the Bates motel, you're wrong.

The scene I'm talking about most viewers don't remember or they ignore. . . . Marion, a real estate secretary working in a Phoenix, Arizona office, steals $40 thousand in cash from one of her boss's clients. Her motive? She wants to begin a better life with her married lover Sam Loomis (John Gavin) in California. That afternoon she drives off to the Golden State, the stolen cash in her purse. Night arrives. Tired and frightened, she pulls her car over to the side of the road and falls asleep. Daytime arrives. A patrolman (an uncredited Mort Mills, a terrific character actor) knocks on her car window and wakes her up.

Patrolman: Hold it there. In quite a hurry?

Marion: Yes. Uh—I didn't mean to sleep so long. I almost had an accident last night from sleepiness. So, I decided to pull over.

Patrolman: You slept here all night?

Marion: Yes. As I said, I couldn't keep my eyes open.

Patrolman: There are plenty of motels in this area. You should've—I mean just to be safe.

Marion: I didn't intend to sleep all night! I just pulled over. Have I broken any laws?

Patrolman: No, ma'am.

Marion: Then I'm free to go?

Patrolman: Is anything wrong?

Marion: Of course not. Am I acting as if there's something wrong?

Patrolman: Frankly, yes.

Marion: Please—I'd like to go.

After the patrolman checks Marion's driver's license, she drives away and he does, too, though at first it seems as if he's following her.

That's the scene: so eerie, nightmarish; the big looming patrolman, his eyes covered by those horrific sunglasses—Oh those SUNGLASSES! Hitchcock's great visual sense is at its peak when Mills' patrolman makes his appearance in the film. The surreal image could be titled "Patrolman Wakes Up Sleeping Woman in Her Car and Questions Her." I bet the patrolman wears them to frighten people he knows have something to hide. That scene bothered me when I first saw it—still does. My advice is never trust anyone whose eyes you can't see.

Think back to the patrolman's suggestion to Marion that *there are plenty of motels in this area. You should've — just to be safe.*

Motels? One of them is the Bates Motel, where that evening Marion stops and meets Noman Bates. At first, he's very polite. Safe? She rents a room at the motel and soon, as Edward White writes in *The Twelve Lives of Alfred Hitchcock,* "Norman Bates' rage tumbles out in explosions of ham-fisted brutality."

But imagine if the patrolman had said, "Check out the motels, miss, but stay away from that Bates place because its owner, Norman, is creepy." Imagine if Marion had taken his advice and gone elsewhere for lodging, the next morning she'd be on her way to California, showered, freshly scrubbed, and refreshed, and she'd find her lover and they'd live happily ever after, though the movie would've turned into a sappy love story and a search for her and the missing money. And good old Normie Bates would continue being good old Normie Bates.

2

An example of an actor people saw on the big and small screens countless times but probably didn't know his name is Mort Mills, Hitchcock's patrolman. He was born Mortimer Michael Kaplan in New York City, New York, in 1919, and appeared in close to 150 movies and television episodes during a twenty-plus year career.

Spell his name after me: M-o-r-t M-i-l-l-s.

THE HARTFORD WHALERS . . . LIKE FAMILY

I am very pleased and honored I could go out there and give the Hartford fans the very best game I could. . . . I have so many great memories going against the Whalers. . . . Over the years, we had some great battles.

— Patrick Roy, retired NHL goaltender

1

Four of us were season tickets holders for the last thirteen years of the Hartford Whalers' existence in the National Hockey League. A friend and I were in attendance at the Hartford Civic Center for the weekend games, and the other two mates were on hand for the weekday battles.

Reading the memorable, much needed history of the Whalers, *The Hartford Whalers: The Rise, Fall, and Enduring Mystique of New England's (Second) Greatest NHL Franchise* by Pat Pickens, set my mind ablaze with memories of the team that joined the NHL on June 22, 1979, along with Edmonton, Quebec, and Winnipeg, and after the 1997 season left for Carolina to become the Carolina Hurricanes.

Pickens writes about the team's key games, the parade in Hartford after the team's elimination by the Canadians in the 1985-86 Adams Division finals, the franchise's miserable trades, its many coaches and players and front office bigwigs, the Carolina Hurricanes, and an enlightening take on why an NHL team hasn't returned to Hartford.

2

I narrowed my memories about the Whalers down to four, though there were close to 6,007 to choose from. Honest!

One: The 1985-86 season was the best in Hartford's history. They finished fourth in the Adams Division with a record of 40-36-4 for eighty-four points. (Yes, I'm aware many fans would argue that the 1986-88 season was Hartford's best ever.)

In the Adams Division semi-finals, the upstart Whalers beat the favored Quebec Nordiques in three straight games. Then, in the Adams Division finals, they faced the Montreal Canadiens. Overtime of the seventh game was when Claude Lemieux, who during the previous six games had scored three goals, struck!

Pickens writes: "[Lemieux's linemate Mike] McPhee drove the net on [Hartford defenseman Tim] Bothwell], pushing him into [goaltender Mike] Liut, and while that was happening, Lemieux shook off Hartford forward Paul MacDermid from behind the goal, took the puck on his backhand, and walked to the front of the net." Lemieux fired "a backhand shot at Liut. Ordinarily, Liut would have covered the top corner, but because of the heavy traffic, Lemieux's shot eluded the netminder and found the back of the net for the game-winning goal at 5:55."

Two: My mind often flits back and forth to some of the team's front office bigwigs — General Manager Ed Johnson, who went from Pittsburgh to Hartford and back to Pittsburgh; GM and team president Emile Francis, who was a genuine hockey man and, Pickens writes, "the architect who had turned a 19-54-7 team into the [1986-1987] Adams Division champions". Team owner Richard Gordon, who wasn't a hockey person and whose micromanagement style eventually dismantled the team; GM Brian Burke, a hockey person who wanted "to toughen the organizational perception and pulled the [Brass Bonanza], Hartford's iconic theme song," and later got rid of the its mascot, Pucky the Whale, and double shame on you, Brian Burke. Team owner Peter Karmanos, who was a hockey person and said he'd give the franchise four seasons in Hartford, which he did.

Three: I won't fault Pickens for not including Tony Harrington in his book because it's impossible to include every person and event associated with the team. An integral part of Hartford's mystique, Harrington sang, in terrific fashion, the Star-Spangled Banner before each home game. And he was there to sing the Anthem for the team's final game in Hartford on that sad Sunday afternoon.

Four: Defenseman Zarley Zalapski . . . He came to the Whalers in the 1990-91 Ron Francis trade and played with the team for four seasons. A skilled, smooth skater, he scored twenty goals in his first season with Hartford.

Hartford fans didn't appreciate Zalapski. The vast majority of hockey fans are decent people, but there are always a few arseholes at every game. (True in any sport, right?) Those jerks would take out their innumerable frustrations on various Hartford players, which often included Zalapski.

Early in October 2017, Zalapski, who played in 637 NHL games, scored ninety-nine goals, and had 285 assists during a career that went from 1987 to 2000, was diagnosed with a viral infection. After treatment, his condition improved and a few weeks later he was released from the hospital. Because of heart complications from the viral infection, Zalapski passed away in his sleep on December 10, 2017, in Calgary, at the age of forty-nine.

Travel well, Zarley.

3

Sunday afternoon, April 13, 1997, as we know, was the last game the Whalers played in Hartford. The opposing team was the Tampa Bay Lightning, and before a sell-out crowd the Whalers skated to a 2-1 victory, as long-time fan favorite Kevin Dineen scored the winning goal.

Seconds after the game ended the Whalers saluted the crowd at center ice with raised sticks and then, in a spontaneous gesture, flipped pucks and equipment into the stands as the Brass Bonanza rocked the Civic Center.

About a month after the final game, I met one of my former community college students by accident at a local restaurant. He was probably in his late-twenties and a loyal fan of the Whalers since the team's arrival in Hartford. We began talking about the team, and he told me when he was eight years old, he, his father, and his grandfather attended almost every Hartford home game.

The threesome would dine out before the game. Family nights never to be forgotten.

With pride he said, "I grew up with the Whalers," as did, I've learned, many other fans of the team.

He added that when his grandfather was in the hospital dying—which was in the early 1990s—he insisted that as long as he was breathing, his grandson and son were to bring the *Hartford Current* with them to the hospital the morning after a Hartford game, home or away, so he could read about it.

I greatly admire the young man, his father, and his grandfather's loyalty to the Whalers. Who wouldn't? On the other hand, what disturbs me are people—and I've met a few—who refuse to understand that for many of the team's fans, the Whalers were more than a hockey team.

BOXING MEMORIES

What makes Jerry Fitch and John J. Raspanti's *A Few More Rounds: A Collection of Boxing Memories* such an engaging, highly readable book is its authors' ability to impart their passion for and knowledge of the sweet science. As longtime boxing journalist/historian Nigel Collins rightly says in his Foreword, "[It's written] by two writers who are keeping the flame of boxing burning bright."

In the chapter titled "My Favorite Fighters," one of Fitch's favorites was Emile Griffith, who fought from 1958 to 1977. A boxing historian and the author of numerous boxing books, Fitch writes about Griffith's 1967 to 1968 classic trilogy against Nino Benvenuti: "Emile lost the middleweight title, won it back from Nino, and eventually lost the third bout to the handsome Italian, all three bouts by decision."

Another classic Griffith trilogy was against Benny "Kid" Paret. In their first encounter in 1961, he halted Paret in the thirteenth round to win the welterweight title. That same year, in their rematch, he lost the title by decision.

In 1962 Griffith regained the crown by stopping Paret in round twelve. As boxing fans know, Paret "was taken out of the ring on a stretcher" and "died ten days later without ever regaining consciousness." For the rest of his life, Griffith was haunted by the Paret tragedy.

Welterweight title! Middleweight title! Junior Middleweight title! The great Griffith was champion in those divisions. When he retired, he had compiled an 85-24-2 (twenty-three KOs/KO by two) record.

In Fitch's piece, "Often Forgotten Middleweight Contenders from the 1950s," he writes that "I went through *The Ring* magazine ratings from the 1950s and picked a dozen of the many forgotten contenders from that time."

Two of them were Ernie "The Rock" Durando and Gene "Silent" Hairston. Durando fought the best middleweights of the time and possessed a devastating right cross. It's an understatement but his four fights against Paddy Young in Madison Square Garden were wars. (Durando's record against Young was 1-2-1, and each fight went the distance.)

Riot anyone? Well, that's what happened during Durando's nationally televised 1952 fight in the Garden against Rocky Castellani. In the seventh round Durando floored Castellani. Back on his feet at the count of nine, Castellani appeared unhurt and ready to continue, but referee Ray Miller thought otherwise and stopped the fight. Enraged by the stoppage, Castellani's manager jumped into the ring and went after Miller, who fended him off with a series of left jabs until security intervened.

The popular Durando, who hailed from Bayonne, New Jersey, was ranked as a top ten middleweight in 1951 and 1952. He began fighting in 1943 and retired in 1957 with a 46-23-4 (thirty-one KOs/KO by six) record.

The crowd-pleasing Hairston, Fitch writes, "became the first deaf fighter to become really known during his career. . . . A red light was put in the corner of the rings he fought in to signal to him that the round was ending."

A ferocious body puncher, Hairston ducked no one. Some of his foes included Bobo Olson, Jake LaMotta, Kid Gavilan, Johnny Bratton, Rocky Castellani, Paul Pender, Charles Humez, Laurent Dauthuille, Paddy Young, and Walter Cartier. And, yes, Hairston deserved a crack at Sugar Ray Robinson's middleweight title, but it never materialized. (I don't think Sugar Ray, great as he was, wanted anything to do with Hairston's thunderous body punches.)

His fight with Cartier has remained in my mind ever since they fought at the Garden in 1951. Hairston floored Cartier once in the first round and again in the second. Body punches. But Cartier made a dramatic comeback and became stronger as the fight progressed, and by round ten Hairston was on the canvas, only to be saved by the bell.

Cartier was awarded a hard-earned split decision.

Hairston fought from 1947 to 1952, retiring with a 45-13-5 (twenty-four KOs/KO by three) record. (I believe he was one of those fighters who fought too often against too many good fighters.)

Turning to Raspanti's "Landmarks and Live Boxing in Carson City, NV" and a fight he saw as a youngster. Accompanied by his father and grandfather, he recalls watching an amateur heavyweight named Peter Wisecarver fight in 1972, at the Tahoe-Carson Speedway in Carson City, Nevada.

"He had Olympic dreams," Raspanti writes. "Every pore of his being seemed to flow with confidence. He looked like a movie star."

And he was "dressed entirely in gold."

His opponent was Jean Mateo, whom "nobody seemed to notice" and whose "trunks were white with a stain in the front." He sat on his stool, and "it looked like his left leg was twitching."

Raspanti, co-author with Dennis Taylor of the critically

acclaimed *Intimate Warfare: The True Story of the Arturo Gatti and Mickey Ward Boxing Trilogy,* writes that mid-way in the round Mateo connected with "[a] long overhand right from downtown Carson [that landed] squarely on the golden one's chin." Down went Wisecarver! The crowd was "in shock and disbelief." Before the round ended, he was dropped two more times. That was it. The referee stopped the fight.

"Ten minutes before [the fight, Wisecarver] had reeked of supreme confidence and acclaim," Raspanti writes. "Now he needed help walking. The crowd ignored him. In the ring, the victor bowed and nodded to the stunned crowd."

Regarding boxing movies, Raspanti says he loved *Rocky* and *Raging Bull,* but "it's the older films that capture the feel of the wicked and brutal world of the red-light sport." He begins his "Five Favorite Must See Boxing Movies" piece with an astute review of Robert Rossen's *Body and Soul,* which starred the great John Garfield as boxer Charlie Davis. Garfield's intense performance earned him an Oscar nomination as 1947's Best Actor.

The final fight scene between Garfield's Davis and Jack Marlow (Artie Dorrell, in real life a professional fighter) "is a mixed bag of betrayal and revenge," Raspanti writes, adding that "cinematographer James Wong Howe filmed the boxing scenes while on roller skates to add realism," an innovative technique that put movie audiences into the ring with Davis and Marlow as they slugged it out.

TEDDY'S ADVENTURES IN TRAINER LAND

1

He's Teddy Atlas and he's authored an unputdownable book written with Peter Alson titled *Atlas: From the Streets to the Ring: A Son's Struggle to Become a Man* (2006). Regarded as one of boxing's most respected trainers, Atlas later became a commentator on ESPN's *Friday Night Fights* (1998-2010).

Atlas was a troubled, violent youth from Staten Island who, when he was eighteen, did time at Rikers Island for armed robbery. But he makes it clear in his memoir that he "grew up in a good neighborhood and lived in a nice house."

In *Atlas: From the Streets to the Ring*, he writes about many significant people in his life, including Twyla Tharp, one of America's greatest ballet dancers and choreographers, and the troubled former heavyweight champion Michael Moorer.

In the early 1980s, Tharp—then forty-four years old, which is old for a dancer— decided to return to performing. "I'd been mostly directing and making dances for others for ten years and found myself woefully out of shape," she writes in *Keep It Moving*. "I had begun to wonder if I would ever be able to really dance again myself."

And guess who she hired to get her back in condition?

Though a friend told Atlas she was "the Muhammad Ali of dance," at first he was reluctant to work with her but, Tharp writes, "I guilted [him] into training a girl."

Atlas told her that "[I'm going to] teach you boxing . . . so that you can learn how to go into dark places and not get broken down. If you can learn a bit of the discipline that fighters learn, you can take that onto the stage with you."

And he wasn't exaggerating about those dark places: "I made her run up and down the steps in the Walker Theater — and there were a lot of steps. I had her skip rope, shadowbox, do push-ups, kick-outs, sit-ups, everything I'd have my fighters do. I ran her ragged, and she dealt with all of it and never complained."

Teddy trained her for about six months.

For the opening of her show in November 1983 at the Kennedy Center, Tharp flew Teddy and Elaine, his wife, to Washington, D.C., to see the performance, which received a standing ovation and critical accolades. As she was taking her bows, Atlas says, she "was looking out at me with this big smile." How did he respond? "I walked up, took a pair of boxing gloves out of a bag I had brought with me, and threw them onstage."

Later, Tharp returned the favor. Moments before one of Teddy's fighters, Simon Brown, the International Boxing Federation world welterweight champion, was going to defend his title, a bouquet of flowers were delivered to Atlas. They were from Tharp.

2

A keen judge of what makes fighters tick, Atlas — before he agreed to train the unpredictable, talented Michael

Moorer for his April 22, 1994, heavyweight title fight against Evander Holyfield at Caesars Palace, Las Vegas—knew "[Moorer] was a guy known as a badass and a trouble-maker. To me, though, it couldn't have been more obvious what he really was: a scared, insecure guy with an inferiority complex and a fear of what he had to do and had to face."

That Teddy didn't have a nervous breakdown training Moorer is amazing because "[every] day was a battle, every day was another test, another challenge, to see if I was going to be there. . . . It got to be very wearing, the physical confrontations, the near fistfights."

The chapters about his relationship with Moorer are among the most fascinating in the book, and though I'm not going to reveal what he did to reach Moorer mentally and physically, Teddy's method was successful: Moorer decisioned Holyfield to become the International Boxing Federation and World Boxing Association heavyweight champion.

After dining with Atlas and his family at their home several days after defeating Holyfield, Moorer presented his trainer with a new Lexus and said, with simplicity and sincerity, "Thank you."

TRADING MIKE ROGERS

Being a small player and not really a physical player by any means, I always relied on my skills and quickness on the ice.

—Mike Rogers, NHL player

After reading *The Hartford Whalers: The Rise and Fall, and Enduring Mystique of New England's (Second) Greatest NHL Franchise* by Pat Pickens, I realized Mike Rogers deserves more recognition than he has received and was someone to write about.

If you want proof, look at his statistics. During the 1979-80 season for the Whalers, he scored forty-four goals and had sixty-one assists for 105 points. In the following campaign he netted forty goals, along with sixty-five assists, again for 105 points.

Before the start of the 1982-83 season, Rogers was traded to the New York Rangers.

Then the hockey gods struck. And I mean struck!

Believe me when I say that no one knew I was planning to write about Rogers. No one except the hockey gods, that is, who made their move on November 8, 2021, moments after I received the latest edition of *The Hockey News*. Glaring at me on pages 92-93 was Ty Di Lello's article about Rogers titled "In Good Company." (Don't tell me the publication of Di Lello's article was some kind of coincidence. No! No! No!)

Di Lello's piece opens like this: "Only four players in National Hockey League history have scored one hundred or more points in each of their first three seasons. Three are easy guesses, but the last will surprise you. The answers: Wayne Gretzky, Peter Stastny, Mario Lemieux, and . . . *Mike Rogers*."

Rogers's reaction: "I'm a pretty good trivia question because nobody ever guesses 'Mike Rogers' when that comes up. But just to be mentioned along those three world-class players is amazing in itself."

The Hartford Whalers joined the NHL in 1979, and when Rogers, who had played four seasons with the World Hockey Association New England Whalers, wasn't claimed by the Vancouver Canucks, he remained in Hartford.

He couldn't be happier because he'd be playing along-side two of his boyhood idols, Gordie Howe and Dave Keon. "What a thrill it was for me to be able to play on the same team and call them my friends," he told Di Lello. "That was the biggest thrill I had playing the game [and] to be able to play with two gentlemen like that was absolutely phenomenal."

Then came the trade to the Rangers, which is just as difficult to understand now as when it happened. Because the five-foot eight-inch, 170-pound Rogers had such impressive back-to-back seasons with the Whalers, "[you'd] think he was a prized possession of the Hartford organization," Di Lello writes. "He was captain of the team, after all."

Turning to Jack Lautier's *15 Years of Whalers Hockey*, the author quotes Doug Sulliman, one of the three players who came to the Whalers from the Rangers for Rogers; Larry Pleau, Hartford's head coach at the time of the trade; and the high scoring Rogers himself.

Sulliman: I think it's a move in the right direction. I'm going to a team that wants and can use me. I'm not happy about leaving New York. . . . If I could pick any place I'd want to be, it's Hartford. It's good to go to a team you can grow with and be a part of.

Pleau: I know Mike Rogers is a popular player with the fans but there is no other way to put it. My job is to develop a team for three or four years from now. There are certain players on a team you can move. Rogers was one who had value. We may never replace the 105 points by him, but we can do other things to improve our club for the future. The trade is in keeping with our philosophy of putting a young, competitive team on the ice.

Rogers: I hadn't been aware of any rumors about getting traded. Then Larry told me I was going to New York. I was mad at first and I wondered why the Whalers would trade me. Larry told me it was because they could get three young players. You know, I'm hardly an old guy myself.

Yes, Rogers had his revenge. "He posted a 103-point season and helped the Rangers reach the second round of the playoffs," Pickens writes. "He scored twenty-plus goals each of his four seasons with the Rangers, and they did not miss the playoffs during his tenure in New York."

In his eight years in the NHL, Rogers tallied 202 goals, and recorded 317 assists, good for 519 points in 494 games. Equally as important as those impressive statistics is that,

Rogers told Di Lello, "[the] fondest thing [about my career] is just how much fun I had playing the game. There was never a day when going to the rink was a chore."

The trade that sent Rogers to the Rangers foreshadowed many of the idiotic trades and front office and coaching changes the Whalers made during their NHL existence.

HE'S WORTH KNOWING

1

Humphrey Bogart's big screen breakthrough was his role as San Francisco private eye Sam Spade in John Huston's *The Maltese Falcon* (1941). According to Jeffrey Meyers in *Bogart: A Life in Hollywood*, "the actor was as eager to play Sam as [George] Raft was to avoid it." Raft sidestepped the movie because he believed it wasn't important and would hurt his career.

The movie, Huston's first directorial effort, begins when Spade and his partner, the swarmy Miles Archer (Jerome Cowan), receive a visit in his office from a woman named Miss Wonderly (an excellent Mary Astor), who, Spade soon learns, also goes by the names Brigid O'Shaughnessy and Miss LeBlanc.

Because of Brigid, or whoever she calls herself, Spade becomes involved with the smooth and sinister Kaspar Gutman (Sidney Greenstreet, his screen debut), the effeminate Joel Cairo (scene stealing Peter Lorre), and a two-bit thug named Wilmer (the always reliable Elisha Cook). Together they're all searching for the Maltese Falcon, a priceless statuette. What a foursome!

2

Later that fog-filled, muggy evening, Archer, who couldn't keep his eyes of Brigid, is murdered.

3

Though the whole movie is one best scene — that's how terrific it is — I'll cite two. First, take what happens in the hallway of the Alexandria Hotel when Spade, on his way to Gutman's apartment, is confronted by the tough talking Wilmer.

> **Spade:** Well, I didn't expect you till 5:25. I hope I haven't kept you waiting.
> **Wilmer:** Keep on ridin' me. They gonna be pickin' iron outta your liver!
> **Spade:** The cheaper the crook, the gaudier the patter, huh? Well, let's go.

A few seconds later Spade easily disarms Wilmer, much to the gunsel's chagrin, and takes him to Gutman's apartment:

> **Spade:** Here. [Handing Wilmer's two guns to Gutman] You shouldn't let him go around with those on 'em. He might get himself hurt.
> **Gutman:** Well, well, what's this?
> **Spade:** A crippled newsie took 'em away from him. I made him give 'em back.
> **Gutman:** By gad, sir, you're a chap worth knowing. An amazing character. Gimme your hat.

Second, take the movie's final scene, also in Gutman's apartment, between Spade and Brigid, who Sam knows has bumped off quite a few people. Watch them carefully because they're two talented actors whose timing and reactions are perfect and believable.

"I don't care who loves who. I won't play the sap for you," Spade says. "I won't walk in Thursby's and I know how many others' footsteps! You killed Miles and you're going over for it."

"Oh, how can you do this to me, Sam?" Brigid says. "Surely, Mr. Archer wasn't as much to you as . . ."

Spade's most important lines in the movie follow, revealing another side of the wise-cracking private eye we're familiar with: We learn he's an honorable man who lives by a code.

"Listen," he says. "This won't do any good. You'll never understand me, but I'll try once and then give up. When a man's partner's killed, he's supposed to do something about it. It doesn't make any difference what you thought of him. He was your partner, and you're supposed to do something about it. And it happens we're in the detective business. Well, when one of your organization gets killed, it's bad business to let the killer get away with it; bad all around; bad for every detective everywhere."

And that the falcon turned out to be fake prompts Brigid to ask Spade that if the statuette had been real and Gutman had paid you, "[would] you have done this to me?"

"Don't be too sure I'm as crooked as I'm supposed to be," Spade, who's never at a loss for words, replies. "That sort of reputation might be good for business—high priced jobs and making it easier to deal with the enemy . . . "

She embraces Sam and kisses him, but there's no way he'll be seduced. No siree. Not our Samuel Spade.

Detectives Tom Polhaus and Dundy arrive and it's curtains for Brigid, a character who stands alongside Angela Lansbury's Eleanor Shaw of *The Manchurian Candidate*, Jane Greer's Kathie Moffett of *Out of the Past*, and Gene Tierney's Ellen Berent of *Leave Her to Heaven* as one of the big screen's all-time wicked women.

Consider what Spade tells her moments after the detectives arrive: "Well, if you get a good break, you'll be out of Tehachapi in twenty years, and you can come back to me." A typical Sam Spade line.

Sometimes all's well that ends well.

CLOUDING MEN'S MINDS

1

In *The Manchurian Candidate* (1962) Sergeant Raymond Shaw—Laurence Harvey, in a stunning, Oscar-worthy performance—returns from Korea and is awarded the Medal of Honor for saving the lives of the men in his platoon. The truth is, they've been brainwashed into believing he saved them.

Shaw, too, has been brainwashed. The Red Chinese programmed him to be an assassin, and when he returns to America his assignment is to kill the Republican party's presidential candidate, allowing its vice-presential nominee to take his place.

The Queen of Diamonds is the trigger. So keep dear Raymond away from a deck of playing cards, okay?

Enter Major Bennett Marco, one of Shaw's few friends. Plagued by recurring nightmares of his imprisonment and torture by the Chinese Communists, Marco vaguely remembers the brainwashing and begins believing that something isn't on the level about what's going on with Raymond Shaw.

The key to the film's emotional punch is embodied by

both Shaw and by his power-mad mother Eleanor Shaw Iselin (Angela Lansbury). Married to right wing senator John Yerkes Iselin (James Gregory), Eleanor, who represents patriotism gone amok and is actively involved with her son's brainwashing, is the power behind her pompous husband's attempt to become his party's presidential nominee.

Lansbury gives the performance of her career: Her glares are menacing, her every word pronounced perfectly and forbiddingly.

Near the end of the movie, before she sends Raymond on his mission to the Republican convention in New York's Madison Square Garden, she tells him, with all the venom and hypocrisy she possesses, that "You are to shoot the presidential nominee through the head, and Johnny will rise gallantly to his feet, and then, with Ben Arthur's body in his arms, stand in front of the microphones and begin to speak. The speech is short, but it's the most rousing speech I've ever read. It's been worked on here and in Russia on and off for eight years. . . . Then Johnny will be in front of those microphones and those cameras with blood all over him, fighting off anyone who tries to help him, defending America even if it means his own death, rallying a nation of television viewers into hysteria to sweep us up into the White House with powers that will make martial law seem like anarchy."

And if you think she's finished you're wrong: "And this is very important. I want the nominee to be dead about two minutes after he begins his acceptance speech. . . . You are to hit him right at the point when he finishes the phrase 'I would not gladly ask any fellow American in defense of his freedom that which I would gladly give myself. My life before my liberty.' Is that absolutely clear?"

What a piece of work wicked Mama Shaw is! (And don't ignore that incestuous kiss she plants on Raymond before he leaves for MSG.)

If you haven't seen the movie, well, no spoilers here, but if you have you know things for team Mama Shaw go haywire at the convention. What happens is horrific!

In the last scene, Sinatra's character, in a chilling tribute to one of filmdom's most doomed characters, has the final say about Raymond, and he delivers his lines flawlessly: "Made to commit acts so unspeakable to be cited here by the enemy who has captured his mind, his soul. He freed himself at last. In the end, heroically and unhesitatingly, he gave his life for his country. Raymond Shaw. Hell. Hell."

2

The film received critical praise, but it was shelved for more than twenty-five years after its release. Roger Ebert wrote that Sinatra, who had a hand in producing the project, battled with United Artists because he believed the "studio was using creative bookkeeping to keep it out of the profit column."

According to its screenwriter George Axelrod, the film was pulled after President Kennedy's assassination: "The climate of the times was such that having an assassination picture floating around seemed to be in grotesque bad taste."

Richard Condon, who wrote the novel on which the movie was based, said that he didn't "think it was ever actually pulled from release. It had begun to peter out and play on late-night television. I know Sinatra has a very high regard for it."

THE PAST IS ALWAYS PRESENT, ISN'T IT?

1

More attention needs to be paid to Pierre Boileau and Thomas Narcejac's 1956 novel *The Living and the Dead*, which Alfred Hitchcock turned into *Vertigo* (1957), one of his best and most mysterious films.

Set in Paris in the early 1940s, the novel begins when Paul Gevigne, a wealthy shipbuilder, asks Roger Flavieres, a Parisian lawyer and former police detective whom he has known for years, to watch Madeleine, his wife, because "[one] thing's certain: Madeleine's no longer the same. . . . the woman living with me isn't Madeleine."

Flavieres discovers that Madeleine's grandmother, Pauline Lagerlac, committed suicide when she was twenty-five (Madeleine's age), and might be taking possession of Gevigne's wife He reluctantly agrees to keep an eye on Madeleine, and after following her to the theater one evening, he becomes romantically obsessed with her: The more he pursues her, the more tortured and uncontrollable his obsession becomes.

1

The first of the novel's three most significant moments occurs when we learn Flavieres blames himself for an incident that happened several months before his meeting with Gevigne. It was on an early summer evening he and a police officer named Leriche were chasing an unarmed criminal who had taken refuge on a sloping roof. Leriche went after the criminal instead of Flavieres, but he slipped and fell to his death.

Flavieres keeps hearing the young officer's scream that "went on and on," the authors write, "passing from a shrill note to a lower one with the distance."

Then he thinks about Gevigne's wife, who also might be "burdened by some gnawing secret, though it couldn't be half as hideous as his. Were her dreams torn by a scream like that? Had she allowed someone to die in her place?"

The novel's second key moment: Flavieres and Madeleine are in the Louvre, and they talk about a town called Saintes:

Madeleine: I must have lived there once upon a time.
Flavieres: When you were a child perhaps.
Madeleine: No. In a former existence.

Outside the Louvre, on the Rue de Rivoli, Flavieres confesses his love for her, and before she leaves in the taxi he has called, he tells her "to stop looking into the past."

The third moment is Madeleine's suicide plunge from a church bell tower in the city of Saint Nicolas. Fearing the worst, Flavieres, though afraid of heights, had chased her up the tower stairs, but she was too far ahead of him to be stopped. Then: "She answered with a shrill cry and a shadow passed across the opening in the wall. Biting his knuckles he counted, as when a boy, between the lightning and the thunder. And the thunder came—a horrid dull thud from below."

Flavieres thinks about Leriche's fall: "Like her, [Leriche] had fallen headfirst. No time to suffer? Really? How could one be sure?" Flavieres realizes Madeleine "would never come back from the nothingness [into] which she had plunged." He blames himself for her death, just as he holds himself responsible for Leriche's.

3

Horrific things happen in the second part of *The Living and the Dead*. After a four-year absence, Flavieres returns to Paris and learns his old friend Gevigne has died in a German air raid. Then one afternoon, while watching a newsreel in a local movie theater, Flavieres sees "[a] woman who turned slowly around and faced the camera." He's positive she's Madeleine Gevigne.

A few days later, in the dining room of the Hotel Astoria, for the second time he sees the woman he believes is Madeleine. The young woman tells him her name is Renee Sourange, but he doesn't, or is *unable*, to believe her—for in his tortured heart and insane mind she's Madeleine Gevigne.

The novel's big reveal occurs when, a few days later in a hotel room at the Astoria, Renee confesses she was Gevigne's mistress and collaborated with him to impersonate Madeleine, for Gevigne needed "someone who would [believe] without question when he said he had already witnessed one attempt of hers to take her life. You're a lawyer . . . and then . . . he had known you so well . . . he knew you'd swallow the story without a murmur."

Then Flavieres learns Gevigne had thrown Madeleine off the bell tower. . . . After so many years he has discovered the truth: That with Renee's help, Gevigne has made him a patsy, a victim of an elaborate set-up.

Here's the thing: He believes Renee is Madeleine . . . and he attacks her, and you want to shout, "Stop, Flavieres! Why are you strangling her if you believe she's Madeleine? Why kill the woman you love?"

After removing his fingers from her throat, he switches on the light and "then uttered a cry which brought people running out of their rooms into the corridor." His last words are the most terrifying and saddest in the novel. After kissing her forehead, he says, "I shall wait for you."

4

Off to the treadmill . . .

I'm back.

Consider the screams in *The Living and the Dead*. There are several of them. Leriche—remember him?—screams as he falls from the roof in pursuit of a criminal. Madeleine screams as she's falling from the church bell tower. After Flavieres choked Renee to death, he screams and people in their rooms hear him and dash into the hotel corridor.

(Gentle reader, if you feel inclined to join the fun, you have my permission to let loose, right now, with a scream or two of your own.)

5

What else is there to say? Well, not much, except that the best thumbnail description of Hitchcock's *Vertigo* I've read is Peter Ackroyd's. In *Alfred Hitchcock: A Brief Life,* Ackroyd writes that the movie—and with a little stretching his explanation applies to Boileau and Narcejac's novel as well—is "about obsession: a man becomes so haunted by what he believes to be the image of a dead woman that he changes the appearance of another woman to resemble her in every detail. They are in fact the same person. . . . Hitchcock was fascinated with obsession, especially that of the male with the female, and it became fruitful territory for exploring some of the more dangerous aspects of sexual fantasy and attraction."

Ah, to be able to write like Mr. Ackroyd.

UP THE CREEK

**[*Schitt's Creek*] is a show [in which] the situations
are truthful and real, so the audiences will invest
emotionally in the characters.**
    —*Eugene Levy, co-creator of* **Schitt's Creek**

Once upon a time, the Johnny Rose family was very rich.
But now they're broke because Johnny's business manager swindled them out of their fortune, and their only
recourse is to relocate from New York to a small town
called Schitt's Creek, which is the title of the Emmy award
winning comedy that aired from 2015 to 2020.

Co-created by Eugene and Dan Levy, *Schitt's Creek*'s
main characters are as follows:

Moira (Catherine O'Hara) is a former soap opera star
who can't stop performing. She's almost always "on." And
those wigs and outfits she wears—wow! There are times
when she hides in her closet, too.

Alexis (Annie Murphy) is an unpleasant brat, but she's
young—early twenties—and there's hope she'll change for
the better, which seems to happen as the show progresses.
Good for her.

David (Dan Levy) is usually grumpy, and he bickers

with everyone. But there's something likeable about him, though you need patience to find it. More, he isn't someone to mope regarding his predicament, which of course was moving from the big city. He and his husband, Patrick Brewer (Noah Reid), become business partners and open Rose Apothecary.

Johnny (Eugene Levy) was the CEO of the financially successful Rose Video. As we know, his manager didn't pay the company's taxes and disappeared, and Johnny and his family were forced to relocate to Schitt's Creek, the town he bought for David on a lark. ("Happy birthday, David. I bought you a town!")

There are times when he's level-headed and understanding, though he's often exasperated by the antics of the Schitt's Creek's denizens, including its mayor, Roland Schitt (Chris Elliot, at his clueless best), and Bob Currie (John Hemphill, almost as clueless as Roland), owner of Bob's Garage. Eventually Johnny becomes co-owner of the Rosebud Motel, which he hopes to develop into a franchise. So maybe he's getting over the trauma of losing his fortune and moving.

Favorite character? For me, it's Mayor Roland Schitt. Check out the following scene between him and Johnny. It's comedy writing and acting at its best.

> **Johnny:** Roland.
> **Roland:** Hey, Johnny Rose. How are you?
> **Johnny:** Fine. Need a big favor.
> **Roland:** Name it.
> **Johnny:** Saturday is Moira's birthday, so we want to throw her a surprise party. So we need an excuse to get her all dressed up and out of the house.
> **Roland:** Dinner at our place. Problem solved.

Johnny: Well, tempting. But it's got to be something fancy and elegant. You know, black tie. So we're thinking maybe Jocelyn is throwing her annual charity fundraiser.

Roland: She hasn't mentioned anything to me about it.

Johnny: Why would she mention it?

Roland: Well, Johnny, if she's planning a fundraiser, I think Jocelyn would mention something about it to her husband.

Johnny: It's not a real fundraiser, Roland. It's just a pretend fundraiser to get Moira out of the house. You see, I could tell her about it myself, but she'd catch on because it falls on the same night as her birthday. She's got to hear about the fundraiser from someone who doesn't know it's her birthday.

Roland: Okay. So then you want me to find somebody who doesn't know.

Johnny: No. I want you to tell her.

Roland: That doesn't make any sense. I know it's her birthday.

Johnny: You only know it's her birthday because I just told you it's her birthday. Moira doesn't know you know it's her birthday.

Roland: I won't tell her.

Johnny: [Becoming annoyed] Why would you tell her?

Roland: I won't tell her. So don't worry about it.

Johnny: Okay. But now I am worried. [Pause] Look. I'm taking Moira out for coffee. We're going up to the café this afternoon and that would be a great time for you to stop by and drop the information

about the fundraiser. [Pause] Tell me you understand the plan.

Roland: [Peeved] Yes, Johnny, I understand the
plan and I don't appreciate being talked to like a
child.

Johnny: I'm sorry. I'm sorry. It's just that this
is so important. This is really important. I want to
make sure you understand the plan.

Roland: I understand all right. [Pause] I just think
it's awfully short notice to start a fundraiser.

Johnny: [Shouting] There is no fundraiser!

Roland: Right. There is no fundraiser.

Johnny [Shouting] It's pretend.

Roland: Pretend. [Shrugs] It's fun time.

Thank you, Roland and Johnny, for that scene. . . . And
could it be that with each episode, the Rose family, though
it confronts a variety of calamities and uncertainties, is
beginning to adjust to life in Schitt's Creek?

Maybe.

CLASS ACT

Tamika Catchings . . . Here are several of her numerous accomplishments on and off the basketball court: She has been a nine-time Women's National Basketball Association (WNBA) all-star; a five-time defensive Player of the Year; the 2012 WNBA's Most Valuable Player; a four-time Olympic Gold Medalist; a member of the Naismith Hall of Fame; named one of the top twenty players in WNBA history.

In 2004, Catchings, who played her entire WNBA career with the Indiana Fever and retired in 2016, created the Catch a Falling Star Foundation, which is aimed at helping disadvantaged children achieve success in life.

Also, she's an author. Written with Ken Petersen, in her book, *Catch a Star: Shinning Through Adversity to Become a Champion*, you'll learn about the abuse she endured during her childhood because she suffered from moderate to severe hearing loss, wore large hearing aids, had a slight lisp, and was shy.

Her mother kept telling her, "There's nothing wrong with you. You'll get through this. You can do anything you set your mind to and work toward." And thanks to Mom, Catchings didn't give up on herself. Pardon the cliché but the rest is history: She became an outstanding collegiate basketball player at the University of Tennessee and later an WNBA superstar.

I want to go back in time to the 2015 season and the Connecticut Sun-Indiana Fever game at the Mohegan Sun Arena. I forgot which team was ahead, but the incident I recall took place in the second quarter.

Under the Sun's basket, players were scrambling for a rebound. The Connecticut team gained possession and were off and running toward Indiana's basket. At the same time the Sun's Kara Lawson had tumbled to the hardwood in front of her team's basket and was writhing in pain.

And I mean writhing!

At Indiana's end of the court a turnover occurred. A Fever player passed the ball to Catchings who was heading full speed toward Connecticut's basket when she saw the injured Lawson.

When a player is hurt timeout is called after someone from the injured player's team has possession of the basketball — but this time it was Catchings who signaled for a stoppage in play. Lawson was attended to by the team's trainer, who helped her off the court and into Connecticut's dressing room for repairs. (She returned to action in the final quarter.)

I'm uncertain if the majority of Sun fans noticed what Catchings did because it happened quickly, but for me it was an act of sportsmanship not to be forgotten.

BARK! BARK! BARK!

Two dogs. One is mine and the other pooch belongs to the neighbors across the street. My mutt is inside, perched on our couch in such a fashion he's able to comfortably look out our front window and bark at the fine-looking Jack Russell mix who can't dash out of his front yard because an invisible fence keeps him where he belongs.

Mr. Russell sports a brown and mostly white coat. Weighs probably thirty to thirty-five pounds. Nice and trim. You see, Mr. Russell hears my dog—his name is Remi— barking. Remi is a lab mix, about five or six years old, black with a white chest (like one of those *Downton Abbey* butlers). He isn't as trim as Mr. Russell and could probably lose about five pounds.

Mr. Russell returns Remi's loud barks, and the back-and-forth battle of the barks goes on for a while.

Here's the rub: Mr. Russell doesn't know where Remi's barks are coming from. Remember: He's outside and Remi is inside, and Mr. Russell is only able to hear him, not see him, which causes him to bark in all directions at the dog who's barking at him. Mr. Russell barks to the left. He barks to the right. He barks at the sky. He barks at the two trees in his yard. He barks at the tree in our yard. He barks at passing cars. He barks at passing birds. He barks at any kid who rides by on a bicycle. If people walk past his house, well, you know what he does.

Remi enjoys Mr. Russell's confusion and will keep barking until I calm him, and once calmed he's clearly aware he has won a unanimous barking decision over Mr. Russell.

Did I mention that Remi is from South Carolina and when he barks, if you listen carefully, you'll detect a pleasant southern accent?

"AW, HORSE FEATHERS!"

1

There's only one Sam Spade and only one Humphrey Bogart, and in the 1941 classic *The Maltese Falcon*, John Huston's first directorial effort, Bogart portrays Spade. You can't ask for anything more in a movie than Bogart as Spade!

Spade's secretary is Effie Perine (Gail Patrick), and he calls her "precious," which she is. After all, she's loyal to him, understands his moods, and is willing to do his dirty work. For example, after Spade's unctuous partner Miles Archer (Jerome Cowan) is murdered, Spade asks Effie to call Iva, Archer's wife, and break the news. He'll keep his distance from the new widow, who, by the way, he has been bedding, though apparently Archer doesn't care.

One more point about Effie: She isn't intimidated by Spade's arrogance. At one point in the movie she's ballsy enough to tell him, "You always think you know just what you're doing, but you're too slick for your own good. Some-day you're going to find out."

Regarding Archer, when Brigid O'Shaughnessy (Mary Astor) appears in Spade's office for the first time, he can't keep his eyes off her. (If there's such a thing as a gawker award, Archer deserves it.)

"Oh, she's sweet," he says to Spade after she leaves. "Maybe you saw her first, Sam, but I spoke first." There's a smirk in his voice.

The night is foggy and clammy and on Bush Street, where Archer has arranged to meet Brigid, he's shot to death. That's it for Cowan's character. Though he appears briefly on screen, he makes a lasting impression on viewers. Good work, Mr. Cowan.

The two detectives, Polhaus and Dundy, are played to perfection by superb character actors Ward Bond and Barton MacLane. As far as Dundy is concerned, Spade is a cheeky bastard, and if he can pin anything on the private eye, he'll relish doing it. (There's one point in the movie when Dundy becomes enraged at Spade and slugs him. Spade is ready to hit back, but Polhaus restrains him.)

Dundy's best line: "It would pay you to play along with us a little, Spade. You got away with this and you got away with that. But you can't keep it up forever." (Straight from Dashiell Hammett's 1930 novel.)

Polhaus, on the other hand, knows how to handle Spade. He's reasonable with him. Doesn't raise his voice. Doesn't threaten him.

There's a standout scene near the end of the movie involving Cairo (Peter Lorre) and Brigid who are fighting in her apartment. Polhaus and Dundy are talking with Spade in the hotel hallway when they hear Cairo scream. They dash inside and separate the combatants. (Brigid was winning the skirmish by scratching, punching, and kicking the perfumed Cairo.)

Dundy wants to know what's going on.

"Aw, wake up, Dundy, you're being kidded," Spade

says. "When I heard the buzzer, I said to Miss O'Shaughnessy and Cairo here, I said, 'There's the police again. They're getting to be a nuisance. When you hear them going, one of you scream and then we'll see how far along we can string 'em, until they tumble.'"

Dundy notices a cut on Cairo's head — one of O'Shaughnessy's punches found its mark — and asks him about it. "The cut," Cairo says. "No. When we pretended to be struggling for the gun, I fell over the carpet. I fell."

Cairo's response prompts Polhaus to voice his best line: "Aw, horse feathers!"

2

If you've read this far in this book, you know from a previous essay titled "He's Worth Knowing" that O'Shaughnessy murdered Archer and a few other people. (Ending people's lives is a hobby with her.)

Astor is convincing in the role of the duplicitous, murderous O'Shaughnessy who lies about everything, including her name. First, she's Miss Wonderly, then Miss Le Blanc, and finally Brigid O'Shaughnessy. And don't forget she has teamed with Kaspar Gutman (Sidney Greenstreet, simply terrific), gangster Wilmer Cook (Elisha Cook), and Cairo in their search for the Maltese Falcon.

And when the statuette is finally in Gutman's hands, lo and behold he discovers it's a fake. Sure, Gutman is upset, but he knows shit happens and life goes on and nothing is going to stop him from finding — someday — the genuine Maltese Falcon. After all, that's his sole purpose in life.

Before he departs from O'Shaughnessy's apartment, he says to Spade, "Frankly, sir, I'd like to have you along.

You're a man of nice judgment and many resources." Then: "Well, sir, the shortest farewells are the best. Adieu. And to you Miss O'Shaughnessy, I leave the Rara Avis on the table as a little memento."

And with a classy, understated flourish he departs to continue his search for the Falcon.

3

O'Shaughnessy's biggest mistake was underrating Spade. At the end of the movie she attempts to seduce him. Doesn't work. He pushes her away and says that she's going to prison for her crimes. (His best line to her, which I quoted in the "He's Worth Knowing" essay, and I'll paraphrase it here, is that if she gets a break and is out in twenty years, he'll be waiting for her.)

Stalwart detectives Dundy and Polhaus arrive and cart her off to the hoosegow, where I bet she tries to seduce the facility's warden. (Any takers?)

4

Turning to director John Huston, who cast his father Walter as Jacoby, the captain of the Palomar passenger vessel. Staggering into Spade's office near the end of the movie, Jacoby drops the statuette he was carrying, sways slightly, and conveniently tumbles onto Spade's couch.

Frightened, Effie asks if he's dead and Spade replies, "Yeah, he couldn't have come far with those holes in 'im."(You can always count on our Samuel Spade to be subtle.)

Walter Huston, who went on to win an Oscar for Best Supporting Actor for his work in 1948's *The Treasure of the Sierra Madre*—his son John directed that one, too—appears on screen for about a minute in *The Maltese Falcon*.

A Huston family joke perhaps.

MOVIE MAGIC OF THE 1940S

It's all so meaningless. Ask yourself what life is all about, whether there's any sense to it or whether it's a stupid blunder?

— Larry Darrell, **The Razor's Edge**

1

Ironically, *The Razor's Edge* is about the evils of greed and materialism, but that didn't stop the bigwigs at Twentieth Century Fox from spending over $1 million — big money back then — making a lavish version of W. Somerset Maugham's novel. After all, business is business.

The star-studded cast includes Tyrone Power as the resourceful, enlightened Larry Darrell; Gene Tierney as the cold-blooded Isabell Bradley; Anne Baxter as the tormented Sophie MacDonald; Clifton Webb as the affected Elliott Templeton; John Payne as the wealthy Gary Maturin; and Herbert Marshall as the sagacious W. Somerset Maugham.

Critical reviews of *The Razor's Edge* were mixed, but with its large cast of established actors, an engrossing soap opera storyline, and Alfred Newman's lush score, it was a perfect fit for the 1940s. Audiences loved it.

2

Maugham's novel, which he said was his last great book, was published in 1944, and the film version released two years later. The main character is Darrell, a returning wounded WWI veteran who drops out of society and wanders across Europe and India to learn about the meaning of life. When he returns to the States — to Chicago — he tries to straighten out the lives of his materialistic, troubled friends.

Power's role is a difficult one. His character makes numerous heartfelt speeches that in the hands of a lesser actor wouldn't be convincing. But he pulls it off: You believe what Darrell espouses because Power doesn't have to act to appear sincere.

For the role of MacDonald, producer Gregory Ratoff suggested Baxter to Twentieth Century Fox kingpin Daryl F. Zanuck. Initially, the cigar smoking Zanuck said no, but Ratoff wouldn't accept his answer and he finally relented.

Baxter knew what the role would do for her career. In her autobiography, *Intermission*, she explained that she approached the role of Sophie as "a secret lark. Not that I didn't concentrate, just that I knew I'd do better if I cared less . . . and treated it like an improvisation."

Baxter's big emotional scene occurs in the hospital when Sophie learns she and her family were involved in an automobile accident, and that her husband and young child were killed, a tragedy from which she never recovered and was the reason she descended into a life of alcohol and prostitution in Paris, where she was viciously murdered, her throat cut.

In *Intermission,* her autobiography, Baxter reveals how she was able to summon up such heartbreaking emotions after being told of her family's deaths. She had been given several weeks off from filming, and when she returned to the set, she learned Power and Tierney had fallen in love, and Webb was giving them expensive parties attended by Marshall and other members of the cast.

That Baxter wasn't invited to the festivities worked to her advantage, she said, because "she brought those emotions of estrangement to her portrayal of the ill-fated Sophie."

Baxter's performance earned her a well-deserved Oscar for the year's Best Supporting Actress.

3

I'm a sentimentalist and for me one of the most memorable scenes in *The Razor's Edge* — it's a favorite movie moment of mine and barely lasts a minute — occurs early on when Darrell arrives at Isabel's house for an evening out. She emerges from her upstairs bedroom, elegance personified, and gracefully walks down the stairs toward the impeccably dressed Darrell, accompanied by Newman's stirring score. In that scene audiences were witnessing Hollywood filmmaking at its romantic best, 1940s-style.

During the 1940s and until his death in the late-1950s, Tyrone Power was Hollywood's handsomest leading man and the Brooklyn-born, green-eyed Gene Tierney one of its most glamorous leading ladies.

JACK DEMPSEY ACCORDING TO DAMON RUNYON AND PAUL DUNCAN

merging from the pages of Damon Runyon's outstanding biography of Jack Dempsey, *A Tale of Two Fists*, is a bigger than life individual who became one of the top ten heavyweight champions of all time.

In his enlightening introduction, Paul Duncan, the book's editor, tells us that in March 1919, Runyon, one of the country's best journalists and short story writers, "returned to America after a six-month stint covering the Great War in Europe, and soon met with Jack Dempsey in Long Beach, New Jersey, to record and embellish Jack's recollections of his past. The life story was serialized over twenty-eight parts from mid-April to mid-June. . . . Often in Dempsey's own words, it is collected here for the first time one hundred years later, together with Runyon's daily reports from Toledo in the days leading up to the [Dempsey vs Jess Willard] fight, as well as its bloody and ferocious denouement."

IN THIS CORNER, WILLIE MEEHAN

When Dempsey retired from boxing in 1927 — he began fighting in 1914 — he had put together a 58-6-9 record. Two of those losses were, as boxing fans know, to Gene Tunney, the first in 1926, the second and more famous because of the long count in 1927.

The other fighters who defeated Dempsey were Jack Downey — it was Dempsey's sixth fight — in 1915; Fireman Jim Flynn, who knocked him out in the first round, in 1917; and crafty veteran Willie Meehan, who posted a 2-2-1 record against the future heavyweight champion during their 1917-1918 rivalry.

In Randy Roberts' *Jack Dempsey: The Manassa Mauler*, we learn that Dempsey's manager Doc Kearns knew his fighter — who was knocking out practically every opponent he fought — needed more recognition, which is why he was matched against the experienced Meehan.

Roberts writes that Meehan was "a 'spoiler,' that breed of fighter who was not of championship caliber but who was difficult and often made a better opponent look bad because he did everything wrong. He was nicknamed the 'Whirling Dervish' because of his penchant for throwing wild punches from odd angles."

The intriguing Meehan — born Eugene Christopher Patrick Walcott on December 25, 1895 — didn't look like a professional fighter. He was "fat [and] had a baby face that made him look like a pugilistic Porky Pig," Roberts writes. "Therefore, audiences usually expected Meehan to be soundly defeated, even though he rarely was."

Born in San Francisco, Meehan's boxing career began in 1909, and he retired in 1926 with a record of 89-29-40. (Almost half of his losses came at the end of his career.)

JOE BONDS, MEET JACK DEMPSEY

Consider the time that the young, upcoming Dempsey fought Joe Bonds, a big, experienced heavyweight from the Northeast with a 24-6-8 record. They met three times, but only once in the ring.

Their first meeting was aboard the train journeying to Ely, Nevada, where their fight would take place. Feasting on several sandwiches, Dempsey ended up sitting next to the big guy:

> **Bonds:** I wonder where a man could get something to eat around here.
> **Dempsey:** Why, I guess there isn't much of any place. Would you like to have a sandwich?
> **Bonds:** Would I? I should say I would. I'm about starved. I'm Mr. Bonds. I'm just back from Australia, and I'm going up here into the sticks to fight some sucker by the name of Dempsey.

Dempsey didn't respond with a big "Hello, Mr. Bonds, I'm Dempsey—Jack Dempsey, your next opponent." He didn't even burp, cough, or grunt. He remained silent.

The train pulled into Ely, and Dempsey headed for Chambers' Saloon to acquaint himself with its owner, Tommy Chambers, who was promoting the fight, and that's where the second meeting between Dempsey and Bonds took place.

When Bonds walked into the saloon, Runyon writes, Chambers immediately introduced him to Dempsey. Bonds, taken by surprise, remembered "what he said about going to fight a 'sucker.'" They shook hands and "no reference to their late companionship" was made.

Their third meeting was inside the squared circle on

August 4, 1916, where Dempsey pounded Bonds for ten rounds. Though Dempsey knocked him down several times, he wasn't able to knock him out. All Bonds did, Dempsey told Runyon, "was holler foul during the fight, and he tore out of town the next day pretty well marked up."

FIXED?

Dempsey and journeyman Fireman Jim Flynn battled two times. In their first encounter, in Murray, Utah — 1917 was the year — Dempsey was stopped for the first and only time in his career.

At the time, Dempsey had fewer than thirty fights, while Flynn fought more than 120 times, including a fight against Jack Johnson.

Was Dempsey's first fight with Flynn fixed? "I have never talked with anyone who had anything more than vague and involved information" about the fight, Runyon writes. For Runyon, what happened to Dempsey was simple to explain: Flynn caught the young Dempsey "on the chin in the first round. Down went Jack like the proverbial log."

Paul Duncan quotes what several sources wrote about the fight. The *Salt Lake Telegram*: "It was the thirteenth day of the month and Jack Dempsey forgot to duck," and "a right hook square on the chin apparently sent Dempsey to the place where the birdies sing, and it was curtains."

The *Salt Lake Tribune*: "During those twenty-five seconds, Flynn punched Dempsey twice on the right side of the head, twice on the left side, broke down Jack's guard with his right, and put the finishing touches on with a steaming wallop with his left to the jaw" and "Dempsey was out for about half a minute."

(According to the *Tribune* it was a left to the jaw that flattened Dempsey; the *Telegram* claimed it was a right hook.)

The *Oakland Tribune*: "The one blotch on Dempsey's list of performances is the fact that he was knocked out by Flynn at Salt Lake. . . . Dempsey never admitted to taking a dive, although several witnesses came forward in 1920."

In their rematch in Fort Sheridan, Illinois, a year later, Dempsey avenged his knockout loss to Flynn by flattening him in one round. Duncan quotes the *Rock Island Argus*: "So Jack was out for the scalp of the Pueblo man and did just what Flynn had done to him, only in a few seconds quicker time."

TRAIN WRECK

Turning to Dempsey's fight with the six-foot six-inch heavyweight champion Jess Willard. The place: Toledo, Ohio. The date: July 4, 1919. The outcome: The twenty-four-year-old challenger demolished Willard, who wasn't able to come out for round four.

In the book's last chapter, Runyon describes how Willard looked after the fight: "He was like a man who had just been pulled from under the wreck of an automobile or railroad train or had met with some other grave accident." But somehow the old champion managed to walk "unsteadily to meet his conqueror" and "congratulate him," because that's "the time-honored custom of beaten ring men."

With Dempsey's victory over Willard, Runyon writes, "The old pugilistic order had changed."

HITCHCOCK'S CAMEOS
AND FAMILY PLOT REVISITED

1

In *The Twelve Lives of Alfred Hitchcock*, Edward White cites the scene in *Lifeboat* (1944) as one of Hitchcock's most creative and unforgettable cameos. "On the page facing the camera is an advertisement for a fictional weight loss product," he writes. "We see two photographs, both of Hitchcock," and "one is his familiar three-hundred-pound self, the other a much slimmer man." Hitchcock had been dieting and "he used *Lifeboat* as a way of advertising that fact to the public."

Thanks to Jane F. Sloan's invaluable *Alfred Hitchcock: A Guide to References and Resources*, here's a sampling of Hitchcock's other cameos: In *Shadow of a Doubt* (1943), he's playing cards on a train. In *Notorious* (1946), he's a man drinking champagne. In *Dial M. For Murder* (1954), he's a man in a school reunion photograph. In *Rear Window* (1954), he's winding a clock in the composer's apartment. In *Vertigo* (1959), he's walking on the sidewalk carrying a horn case. In *Psycho* (1960), he's wearing a Texas hat outside the realty office where Marion Crane works. In his last movie, the comedy-thriller *Family Plot* (1976), he's seen behind a door marked "Register of Births and Deaths."

Hitchcock's appearances, as White believes, are "life intruding on art," but there are, of course, several other interpretations. For example, they're his way of having fun with the audience; after all, it's well known he possessed a playful sense of humor. They're a reminder to viewers that he's the director of the film they're watching — in other words, "it's only a movie," as he once said. They're also his way of showing that he's an entertainer. (Want proof? Check out his TV stint as host of *Alfred Hitchcock Presents*.)

And the first cameo Hitchcock made lasted about fourteen seconds. The movie was 1937's *Young and Innocent*.

1

According to Donald Spoto in *The Art of Alfred Hitchcock*, 1976's *Family Plot* "has an extraordinary youth and zest" and "was a small but significant gem." The setting is probably San Francisco, and the wealthy Julia Rainbird (Cathleen Nesbitt) hires a spiritualist named Blanche Tyler (Barbara Harris) to find her lost nephew, the illegitimate son of her late sister and her only surviving heir. He has a fortune coming to him.

"I am seventy-eight years old," she says to Blanche, "and I want to go to my grave with a quiet conscience." If Blanche and her boyfriend, cab driver and aspiring actor George Lumley (Bruce Dern), are successful in finding Rainbird's nephew, they'll be $10,000 richer.

Here's the rub: The lost nephew's real name is Eddie Shoebridge. As a teenager, Spoto writes, "[Eddie] and his crony Joe Maloney had set fire to the Shoebridge home," killing his adoptive parents. The murders were "designed to look as if the boy had died in the blaze too." Eddie Shoebridge changed his name and moved and isn't "in the family burial plot at all."

Enter Fran (Karen Black, terrific as always) and her boyfriend, the immaculately dressed jewelry store merchant Arthur Adamson (William Devane). The twosome make their money by kidnapping prominent people and stealing diamonds.

In typical Hitchcock fashion—that is, by chance—Blanche and George cross paths with Fran and Arthur, and we learn that Arthur Adamson was once the murderous Eddie Shoebridge. Yes, indeed, the past and the present connect in so many Hitchcock movies.

What a foursome! Blanche and George, Fran and Arthur. But there's a difference between them: Blanche and George are small time con artists who are after money but aren't murderers; Arthur has no problem disposing of people who stand in his way, and the weak-willed, pouting Fran goes along with him.

How's this for Hitchcockian irony? As Spoto points out, Arthur doesn't know until near the end of the movie that he's Julia Rainbird's lost heir and worth more money than the ransoms he claims from the people he has kidnapped.

What to look for

First, there's the car chase scene, though in *Family Plot* there's only one car, but every time I see the movie it seems as if two cars are involved, with one chasing the other. The day is sunny. Blanche and George leave Abe and Mabel's Café, where they were supposed to meet Joe Maloney (Ed Lauter, menacingly excellent), but Maloney doesn't appear in the café. On the steep, curving mountain road heading home, Blanche asks why George is driving so fast. Close to panicking, his eyes wide as softballs, he tells her the accelerator is stuck and the brakes won't work, and that Maloney has tampered with them. On their left is a cliff, and George is swerving along the road attempting to avoid it and other cars. Blanche is hysterical, pulling on George's tie, choking him. Finally, he's able to drive off the road into a ditch, where the car comes to a stop on its side. Blanche and George are shaken but okay. Walking away from the car, they see Maloney's car approaching. He offers them a ride, but they refuse. He drives off but soon turns his car around and speeds toward them. They run. Another car appears and Maloney tries to avoid it, but he loses control of his car and over the cliff it goes. Bye-bye, Maloney.

Second, there's the scene during a church service at a downtown cathedral where the bishop is kidnapped. Fran walks in front of the bishop, who has been conducting the service, and pretends to faint. Disguised in priestly robes, Arthur appears, walks rapidly to the bishop who's leaning over, and jabs a needle into his arm. Arthur and Fran rapidly escort the barely conscious bishop from the cathedral as the astonished congregation watches. The kidnapping happens fast—Hitchcock fast!

Driving away from the cathedral with the bishop now unconscious in the back seat, Fran admits to Arthur that she was frightened, fearing that the worshippers would come to the bishop's assistance. Arthur's smug response is that the reason no one helped the bishop is because "[people] in church are inhibited" and "too religiously polite."

Third, consider *Family Plot*'s structure: The movie begins with a close-up of Blanche at Julia Rainbird's home, and at the end comes full circle with another close-up of her—only this time she grins and winks at the camera.

"HE KEEPS COMING BACK"

1

W.K. Stratton's *Floyd Patterson: The Fighting Life of Boxing's Invisible Champion* is an informative, thoroughly researched, and exceptional biography of the late, enigmatic two-time world heavyweight champion, who began boxing professionally in 1952 and retired in 1972 with a 55-8-1 (forty KOs/KO by five) record.

(Such fast hands. Such a devastating left hook.)

Some of his achievements: In the 1952 Summer Olympics, he won a gold medal fighting as a middleweight. As a professional fighter, at the age of twenty-one, he became the youngest boxer in the sport to win the heavyweight championship, and he was also the first heavyweight to regain the title after losing it.

And his career shouldn't be defined by his two losses to Sonny Liston and even by his trilogy with Sweden's Ingemar Johansson, with whom he later became good friends.

2

When he was growing up in Brooklyn, Patterson was a bullied, troubled, and extremely shy youngster. As a teenager, he began skipping school and stealing from local stores. Jail would've been his next stop, but fortunately common sense prevailed, and he was sent to Wiltwyck School for Boys in upstate New York. It was a life-changing experience for him.

A Wiltwyck teacher named Vivian Cohen, Stratton writes, "became one of the most people important in Floyd's life." What she did with Patterson and many of the other boys at the school was bring "them out of their shells and convince them that they could learn," and soon Patterson became one of "the bright lights of Wiltwyck."

3

Patterson possessed an innate sense of decency and sportsmanship that often manifested itself, to the chagrin of many old-time boxing fans, in the squared circle. In 1953, for example, in his fifth professional fight, he battled journeyman Chester Mieszala at the Chicago Stadium. In an early round, a hard right hand to Miezsala's jaw sent his mouthpiece flying.

"Unbelievably," Stratton writes, "Mieszala stopped fighting, bent over, and tried to retrieve [it] from the canvas." And just as unbelievable was Patterson's reaction: He stopped punching and "joined Mieszala in an attempt to retrieve the piece of gear. Finally, the referee called time-out and re-inserted the mouthpiece himself."

In 1961, after knocking out Ingemar Johansson in their

third fight, Patterson "did something no one could ever remember seeing in a boxing ring before. He kissed Johansson on the cheek after his defeated opponent stood back up." Later he explained that "it was my expression of admiration for a man who had fought me so well."

When he fought Henry Cooper in London, in 1966, he "helped Cooper up from the mat after the referee called an end to the bout," and "was apologetic about the cut he gave Cooper on the side of his nose."

4

Patterson was no stranger to racial prejudice. After he knocked out Archie Moore in the 1956 heavyweight title elimination bout at the Chicago Stadium, he took part in a series of exhibition bouts, the last one being held in segregated Fort Smith, Arkansas, the state where Orval Faubus was governor.

"Patterson arrived at the Fort Smith station to find an 'all white reception committee' waiting for him," Stratton writes. "They glared as he stepped onto the platform, then formed a semicircle to block his path." That's when Father Sam J. Delaney of the city's St. John the Baptist Catholic Church "waded through the crowd and introduced himself to Patterson" and "offered to transport [him] and those traveling with him into town."

When Patterson appeared at the arena that night, he "realized that he was performing before a segregated audience. Every face he saw was white. The crowd was well-enough mannered, though subdued." There were, however, "blasts of enthusiastic cheers coming from somewhere in the distant shadows of the big room. Later, Patterson learned they were from a single, remote section of seats where black fans were allowed to sit."

That was the moment when "Patterson resolved he would never again fight at a venue that was not fully integrated."

5

Stratton sheds new light on Patterson's relationship with Muhamad Ali. Several days before their second fight at Madison Square Garden for Ali's North American Boxing Federation title, in 1972, the champion said, "I thought [Patterson] was finished. But like a ghost he keeps coming back. It's something to see him still going like he is. He came back after Johansson, he came back after Liston, he came back after Quarry, he came back after me. . . . He still says Clay, but I can't even get mad at him, he's so nice. Everybody else calls me Muhammad and he calls me Clay. He's the only one who can get away with it."

Ali won their second fight, when Patterson's corner wouldn't allow him to come out for round eight. After the fight, Patterson, professional boxing's exemplary gentleman, retired without fanfare.

WHAT INTERESTED ME MOST...

. . . **about** Roger Kahn's anthology *Beyond the Boys of Summer* (2005), edited by Rob Miraldi, was Part VI, "On Getting Old," which includes five journalistic pieces about — you guessed it — getting old.

In "The Young Writer Meets the Aged Poet," the thirty-three-year-old Kahn interviewed Robert Frost, then eighty-six, at the poet's Vermont home. Regarding poetry, Frost said, "I never like to read anyone who seems to be saying, 'Let's see you understand this, you damn fool.' What's a poem if it is not to share with others? But I don't like poems that are too personal. The boy writes that the girl has jilted him, and I know who the boy is and who the girl is, and I don't want to know."

More: "What some seem to do is worry a thing into shape and have others worry with them. Not to say I don't have the distress of failure, but the worry way isn't for me."

"And what makes a good poem?" Kahn asked. Frost's response was that "any good poem is not made. It's born complete."

When he and Kahn took a break from the interview and went outside — it was early afternoon and "the grass looked bright and fresh" — Frost, who prided himself on his athletic abilities when he was a young man, told Kahn that he "used to play softball out past there. I pitched. They don't let me do the things I want to anymore, but if we had a ball, I'd pitch to you a little, and I'd surprise you."

. . . **about** *Lena* — which Lena Horne, a national treasure, wrote with Richard Schickel — was a 1960 incident in which she was involved that took place at the Luau Restaurant in Beverly Hills, California. A drunk wanted immediate service, but the waiter patiently explained that he was serving Horne's table.

The drunk replied, "So what?" Then he shouted a racial slur and bellowed, "Where is she?"

Horne jumped to her feet, grabbed the table lamp, held it in front of her face, and said, "Here I am, you bastard. I'm the nigger you couldn't see," and "I started throwing things [at him]. The lamp, glasses, an ashtray. I'm an excellent thrower."

The ashtray found its target — the arsehole drunk's forehead.

Horne's husband, Lenny Hayton, restrained her until the police arrived and removed the bleeding man from the restaurant, who was later identified as vice-president of an engineering firm.

What Horne had learned from her grandmother and father, early in her life, kicked in that night at the Luau, which was, she writes, "not to take any nonsense from anybody. They had instilled enough of a snob in me to make me believe I was as good as anyone else."

. . . **about** Jerry Stiller and Fred Willard was their wonderful gift — which came directly from the comic gods — of making people laugh. Stiller, ninety-two, passed away on May 11, 2020, and Willard, eighty-six, on May 15, 2020.

Stiller is best known for his roles as Frank Costanza on *Seinfeld* and Arthur Spooner on *The King of Queens,* and I'll do some bragging now and say that atop one of my bookcases is an autographed 8x11 photograph of Stiller. Somehow several years ago I found his address, mailed him a letter requesting a photo and wishing him a Happy Festivus. (A what?)

Five days later Stiller's signed photograph arrived.

There were many Frank Costanza moments to enjoy on *Seinfeld.* One of them was when he explains the Costanza family holiday—it's called Festivus and celebrated on December 23—to Jerry Seinfeld's bizarre next-door neighbor and friend Cosmo Kramer.

Frank: Many Christmases ago I went to buy a doll for my son. I reached for the last one they had, but so did another man. As I rained blows upon him, I realized there had to be another way.

Kramer: What happened to the doll?

Frank: It was destroyed. But out of that a new holiday was born. Festivus for the rest of us!

Kramer: That must have been some kind of doll.

Frank: She was. At your Festivus dinner you gather your family around and tell them all the ways they have disappointed you.

Kramer: Is there a tree?

Frank: No. Instead there's a pole. Requires no decoration. I find tinsel distracting. [Pause] Festivus is back.

In her tribute to Stiller, Leah Remini, who worked with him for nine years on *The King of Queens,* said, "I will be forever grateful for the memories, the fatherly talks off screen, and for the many years of laughter, the kindness he had shown to me and my family. You will be so very missed, Jerry."

Fred Willard's career spanned fifty years and included numerous television appearances, most recently on *Modern Family*, and movies like *This Is Spinal Tap*, *A Mighty Wind*, and his signature performance as a clueless dog show commentator in 2000's *Best in Show*. I'm sure anyone who saw *Best in Show* can't forget what Willard's Buck Laughlin said to the TV audience after he watched each prize dog being examined: "I don't think I could ever get used to being poked and prodded like that. I told my proctologist one time, 'Why don't you take me out to dinner and a movie sometime?'"

"[Fred's] immense talent and kindness will never be forgotten," Christina Applegate, who co-starred with Willard in the movie *The Legend of Ron Burgundy*, said. "We love you, Fred Willard. Thank you for decades of laughter."

... **about** 1987's *Moonstruck*, a lovely modern movie fairy tale, is the final scene. That's when the cast has gathered together in the Castorini's kitchen, and Cosmo Castorini's father, played to perfection by Russian actor Feodor Chaliapin, utters perhaps the movie's most memorable line. It consists of two words.

After the verbal gymnastics about Johnny Cammareri not marrying Loretta Castorini, Cosmo's daughter, and Ronny Cammareri, Johnny's brother, proposing to the widowed thirty-something year old Loretta and her accepting, and Rose Castorini, Loretta's mother, responding "Oh God, that's bad" — well, the old man reacts by crying. When Cosmo asks him what's wrong, he tearfully replies, "I'm confused."

What's more rewarding than a movie about an Italian family directed by Norman Jewison who's Jewish, and written by John Patrick Shanley who's Irish?

. . . **about** the prolific Mark Alan Baker's *Lou Ambers: A Biography of the World Lightweight Champion and Hall of Famer*, are two scenes. One is heartbreaking and the other a comical word picture to savor.

Born Luigi Giuseppe d'Ambrosio, Ambers grew up in Herkimer, New York. Early in his career, he boxed under the names of Lou Ambers and Otis Paradise. He was world lightweight champion in the late-1930s, and he retired in 1941 with an astounding 90-8-6 (thirty KOs) record.

That said, on March 17, 1936, Ambers experienced what every fighter dreads. He knocked out his opponent, Tony Scarpati, in the seventh round at New York's Broadway Arena. Scarpati, twenty-two years old, died three days later.

Ambers was devastated and "could hardly speak [about what happened] without breaking down," Baker writes. A decent and respectful man, he approached the Scarpati family and asked for permission to attend their son's funeral. The family agreed, and then "Ambers was led to a room where Mrs. Scarpati was mourning. Arising from a chair, her face dampened with fresh tears, she opened her arms and embraced the fighter as if he was her own son."

A devout Roman Catholic, Ambers "wrestled with the consequences of the [Scarpati tragedy]" and sought counsel from Father Gustave Purifacato, his longtime friend and spiritual advisor.

On a lighter note, take Baker's vivid and hilarious account of writer Damon Runyon's meeting in the late-1930s with Ambers' manager Al Weill, who later managed many ranked fighters, including heavyweight champion Rocky Marciano.

They met at Weill's favorite Italian restaurant, and as Weill was readying to leave he spotted Runyon seated not far from him. "Runyon, who would rather choke on his bread stick than chat with Weill, did his best to blend into the contrasting tablecloth — you know, one of the white and red checked variations," Baker writes. "But the wordsmith had no such luck. Weill, complete with dangling fragments of Italian bread, pasta e fagioli, and a lone toothpick bobbing at the corner of his mouth, began pontificating about fighting styles. Runyon, who had no idea what Weill was talking about, attempted a level of clarification through questioning his visitor. Finally, it became clear that the former promoter was comparing the styles of Joe Louis and Max Schmeling."

The author of twenty books, seven of them about boxing, Baker is currently working on a book about Ernest Hemingway.

... **about** *Land* are, first, star and director Robin Wright's character, Edee; and second, the final meeting between Edee and Miguel.

Edee has suffered a horrific tragedy in her life — the murder of her husband and young son — and hopes to cope with the tragedy by breaking away from society and buying a run-down cabin on a Wyoming mountain, where she'll self-isolate. But life on the mountain is much more difficult than she expected, and she would've died if it hadn't been for a local hunter named Miguel Borras (Demian Bichir) and a nurse named Alawa Crowe (Sarah Dawn Pledge).

When she asks Miguel how he found her, he replies, "You were in my path."

Land's most indelible scene occurs near the end of the movie when Edee, who's ready to leave the mountain and return to society, visits Miguel at his home. There, she learns he's dying of cancer and also about a terrible tragedy in his life that he holds himself responsible for: Several years ago he was driving drunk, crashed his car, and his wife was killed.

When Miguel tells her, "I'm glad you made it so I could thank you," she replies, "Me?" Then she thinks, *Why are you thanking me? I should be thanking you for saving my life.*

What he says next is the movie's most profound line: "You gave me all I wanted. You offered me a way to die in a state of grace."

HITCHCOCK'S ANN TODD IN CLOSE-UP

1

Donald Spoto writes in *The Art of Alfred Hitchcock* that 1947's *The Paradine Case* "may be one of [Hitchcock's] films most in need of reassessment and fresh appreciation" and "if we take the movie on its own terms, it rewards richly." As usual he's correct.

In *The Paradine Case* barrister Anthony Keane (Gregory Peck) becomes romantically and blindly obsessed with his client, the elegant and mysterious Maddalena Paradine (Alida Valli), who's on trial for murdering Colonel Richard Paradine, her blind husband. (She's accused of poisoning the chap.)

Keane attempts to pin the murder on the Colonel's man-servant Andre Latour (Louis Jourdan, his movie debut), with whom Mrs. Paradine had an affair.

One more thing about Mrs. Paradine: Before she went on trial, she told Keane that as a young woman she had an affair with a married man. When he asked her if there were others, she responded, "Of course there were others. We cannot hide these things."

2

What to look for

First: Take the scene when Mrs. Paradine is in the witness box, and she and everyone in the courtroom learns that Latour has committed suicide. Lashing out in anger, she replies, "What does it matter now? Andre's dead. The man I love is dead. . . . Andre wouldn't help me. . . . Andre knew I killed the blind man. Andre knew it. I didn't tell him. He knew it."

Then she verbally attacks Keane: "I have nothing more to say to you, Mr. Keane. I loved Andre Latour, and you murdered him. My life is finished. It is you yourself who have finished it. My only comfort I have is the hatred and contempt I feel for you."

Visibly unnerved by the news of Latour's death and Mrs. Paradine's confession of guilt, Keane, standing up, addresses the court: "My Lord and members of the jury, I've done my best. This case has already taken its heavy toll on me in the light of Latour and its burden on you. I-I am more than ever conscious of my shortcomings. Everything that I have done seems to have gone against my client. . . . You must not confuse my incompetence with the issues of the trial. . . . I regret that I cannot go on any longer."

He turns the case over to his colleague, Mr. Collins, and leaves the courtroom, head bowed. Like James Stewart's Scottie Ferguson of Hitchcock's *Vertigo*, Keane is a broken man.

Second: There's the last scene involving Keane's wife Gay, compellingly played by Ann Todd, that takes place at the Keanes' home after he has returned from the courtroom. In close-up she tells her husband that "it won't be easy. . . I don't think the newspapers will be very kind to you. . . .

Tony, the most important moment in your life wasn't when you discovered what she was." You were, she continues, courageous to apologize to the court for being wrong about Mrs. Paradine, but "the most important moment in your life is now. My husband is the most brilliant man I've ever known. . . . I want you back on the job just as fast as you can."

In that difficult scene, Todd was able to deliver her lines convincingly because Hitchcock put her at ease. Todd remembers: "He takes the trouble to study his actors quite apart from what they're playing, and so is able to bring hidden things out of them. He always realized how nervous I was and used to wait for the silence before 'Action' and then tell a naughty, sometimes shocking story that either galvanized me into action or collapsed me into giggles: either way it removed the tension."

Gay still loves her husband and believes in his future as a lawyer, but the question is can he regain his sense of self-esteem as barrister and husband, or is he as completely crushed as Ferguson is at the end of *Vertigo*?

THE AMAZING HARRY GREB

A unique style is very important in becoming a champion. I think Harry Greb's boxing will best illustrate this. . . . There was never a man who typified Harry's style of boxing. He threw punches from every angle. He rained uppercuts and blows that were used by no other boxer. He had a great faculty for starting a blow and stopping it in midair, but countering with another blow. I should say that the greatest I ever fought was Greb.

—Pal Reed, middleweight who fought Harry Greb twice

1

Of the five myths concerning Harry Greb, which Bill Paxton examines in his excellent book *The Fearless Harry Greb: Biography of a Tragic Hero of Boxing,* the two most important are his last name and his eyesight.

In the chapter titled "The Myths Grow While the Legend Fades," Paxton explains that "a year after [Greb's] death, a sportswriter made up a story that the real name on his birth certificate was 'Berg.' The story goes that Greb thought the name sounded too Jewish and might have cost him some fans and boxing engagements."

Correcting matters was a 1954 magazine article titled "Harry Berg or Harry Greb" that printed a copy of the fighter's birth certificate and "clearly showed that his last name had always been 'Greb.'"

Paxton adds that "I have spoken with a few of Greb's relatives in Germany and it is very clear that the name was always Greb. His family's U.S. Census results, as well as his birth certificate, all confirm that his name was always Greb." Case closed!

Paxton goes on to shatter the belief Greb fought with a glass eye, though he "did get a glass eye surgically implanted. However, he only had it for the last two months of his life, and Greb never fought while he had a glass eye." Another case closed!

1

Edward Henry Greb was born on June 6, 1894, to German immigrants in Pittsburgh, Pennsylvania. He married Mildred Riley, his childhood sweetheart, in 1917. She died of tuberculosis three years later. They had one daughter, Dorothy.

Greb's professional boxing career began in 1913. Weighing between 160 and 168 pounds, he fought middleweights, light heavyweights, and heavyweights. From 1922 to 1923 he was the American light heavyweight champion and then middleweight title holder from 1923 to 1926.

According to boxrec.com, when he retired from fighting in 1926, he had compiled 108-8-2 (forty-nine KOs/KO by two) record. Other sources claim he fought over three hundred times.

In Paxton's deeply researched biography, which is enhanced by more than 120 photographs, the author covers in detail the life of one of the most amazing prizefighters in the sport's history, a prizefighter who for many boxing scholars and fans is the greatest of all time.

3

Heavyweight champion Jack Dempsey and Greb almost fought in 1919, but the contest "never took place because Dempsey didn't want to fight," Paxton writes. "Dempsey knew it was going to be a tough battle for him to win, and that Greb could win on points. Therefore, he would continue fighting men that Greb had already beaten rather than fight Greb himself." And among those fighters Dempsey fought were Willie Meehan, who beat Dempsey twice, Ed "Gunboat" Smith, Terry Kellar, Jimmy Darcy, Battling Levinsky, Tommy Gibbons, Billy Miske, Joe Bonds, Bill Brennan, and Gene Tunney.

Yes, Dempsey sparred with Greb on July 27, 28, and 29 in 1920. After their third session, Paxton writes, the *Pittsburgh Post* would note that "a big surprise was sprung on those present by the way Greb tore into the champion, and in the middle of the second round, time had to be called when the Pittsburgher landed a hard right on Dempsey's left eye and split it open."

It's generally agreed Greb had the best of his three sparring sessions against Dempsey.

To prepare for his September 6, 1920, fight against Billy Miske, Dempsey again hired Greb as his sparring partner. Their third and final session took place on September 3, and, Paxton writes, "The previous day of sparring took so much out of Dempsey that he only allowed two rounds with Greb."

The *New York Times* reported that "Harry Greb, looking chipper as ever in his U.S. Navy jersey and his black tights, climbed into the ring to take Dempsey over the jumps for two rounds of three minutes each.'"

4

Greb became the American light heavyweight champion when he decisively defeated Gene Tunney on May 23, 1922, at Madison Square Garden. Jack Cavanaugh, in his biography of Tunney, *Tunney: Boxing's Brainiest Champion and His Upset of the Great Jack Dempsey*, writes that "Round after round, Greb, as Hype Igoe would write in his account of the fight, 'came at Tunney from every angle with a thousand gloves laced to each piston-like arm.' It was an apt description, as Greb swarmed all over Tunney refusing to give him adequate punching room and battering him almost at will, to the astonishment of much of the crowd and particularly Tunney's hundreds of supporters from Greenwich Village."

The only fighter to defeat Tunney, Greb went on to fight him four more times. After their last fight Greb spoke to Tunney and told him, "You're ready for anyone now. You'll lick Gibbons and you'll lick Dempsey. I know, I boxed with both of 'em. You got the style to lick 'em. You can't miss, kid, and when you're the big champ, remember it was Harry Greb who told you so."

As we know, Tunney went on to become world heavyweight champion and retire undefeated, which of course was no surprise to Greb, whose record in his five fights against Tunney was 1-3-1.

5

The color line didn't exist for Greb. Paxton writes that "[unlike] many of his fellow white boxers during his time, Greb didn't subscribe to this prejudice; Greb just wanted to get better as a boxer and constantly fight the best. That meant fighting some African American boxers, no matter what some people may have thought about it." (Neither Tunney nor Dempsey ever fought an African American.)

Greb's light heavyweight fight against Kid Norfolk, a future member of the International Boxing Hall of Fame (2007), and a fighter white boxers avoided because of his color and ability, took place on August 29, 1921, at Forbes Field in Pittsburgh. In round three Norfolk dropped Greb with a terrific right hand to the jaw. But as the fight progressed, Greb became stronger — which wasn't unusual for him — and pulled out a close ten round decision.

In one of the book's most important passages, Paxton writes that Greb suffered an eye injury "from a punch in the Norfolk fight. A retinal tear occurred five days later with visual impairment starting up after that. Greb would keep this a secret from the general public for the rest of his life; he would only tell a few close friends and his family."

What exacerbated Greb's eye problem occurred during his November 22, 1922, fight in New York at the Buffalo Auditorium. His opponent, "Captain" Bob Roper, well-known in boxing circles as a dirty fighter, "may have thumbed Greb's eye, which may have worsened Greb's retinal tear and caused a full retinal detachment."

Though he was blind in his right eye, Greb was able to continue fighting because of his unique boxing style. "He was constantly moving, which made it easy for his left eye to constantly see his opponent from different angles. This lessened the number of 'blind spots' due to the loss of vision of the right eye."

In an Atlantic City hospital, on October 21, 1926, Greb went for "his final treatment of the optic, and for what he considered minor injuries" suffered in an early October automobile accident in Pittsburgh," Paxton writes. (The crash was one of several Greb was involved in during his life.)

After an examination at the hospital Greb learned that "his nasal passage had been entirely blocked," and he agreed on "the removal of the fractured bones."

The day after the operation Harry Greb died at 2:30 p.m.

Paxton quotes Dr. Weinberg, who was present during the procedure: "[Greb's] death was due to a blood clot on the brain related to Greb's automobile accident, [and that] evidently a piece of bone extending from the bridge of the nose to the floor of the skull had been fractured in such a manner that a blood clot was formed in the brain."

AMERICA'S GREATEST SPORTSWRITER

1

The most noteworthy aspect of Jack Kerouac's book of previously uncollected writings, *Good Blonde & Others* (1993), is his "little eulogy" of Dan Parker (1893-1967), which appears in the piece titled "The Greatest Sports Writers Who Ever Lived as Far as I'm Concerned."

Kerouac discusses several other writers, including Jimmy Cannon, Frank Graham, and Red Smith. Cannon, he says, "was not so hot as he thought he was because of all his dismal attempts to sound like Hemingway or like Runyon." When Kerouac wants "information," he doesn't read Cannon, but rather "I go to Frank Graham and Dan Parker and Red Smith." (He believes James Daley is "purty good" too.)

Regarding Frank Graham, who, like Parker, should be better known, Kerouac writes he "had a sparse, thin-as-a-rail style that appealed to me simply as reportage devoid of style-consciousness and yet conscious of the quality of what prose should be."

It's Kerouac's hope that "someone will put together Parker's columns in a book," and it's mine, too, because I grew up reading Dan Parker, who spent thirty-eight years writing for the *New York Mirror*, was born in Waterbury, Connecticut, and inducted in 2017 into the Connecticut Boxing Hall of Fame.

Let's do a Ray Bradbury and go back in time to the mid-1950s — to New Haven and Norton Street — when yours truly was an unpredictable ninth grade student at Troup Junior High School. A relative, my uncle to be exact, returning home from work on a Sunday evening at about 11:30 p.m. would always bring a copy of the hot-off-the-press Monday New York *Daily Mirror* with him. He'd give it to me, and I'd immediately turn to Parker's column, which would be about the main event scheduled that coming Friday night at Madison Square Garden, or occasionally at St. Nicholas Arena, the country's oldest fight arena. From Parker I'd get insights of and detailed information about both combatants and who was favored to win and who he thought would win. His predictions were usually spot-on.

I'm going to quote what noted sports journalist Sherm Cain wrote about Parker, because you'll learn he was much more than a sports columnist who wrote about the Friday Night Fights: "Parker would first go on to become a sportswriter of the *Waterbury American*. But he found his niche at the *New York Daily Mirror* where he was known for his articles that exposed the corruption in boxing.

"He earned high praise for exposing the International Boxing Club as a crooked organization that was sullying the name of the sport with its corrupt promotions. The IBC eventually was disbanded in large part due to Parker's crusade.

" . . . his brilliant writings and strong moral fiber was finally recognized by the International Boxing Hall of Fame, which inducted Parker in 1996. He is also in the National Sportswriters and Sportscasters Hall of Fame."

2

Let me digress for a moment . . . In the mid-1950s, a friend and I would occasionally drive on a Monday evening to New York from New Haven. When we arrived in the Big Apple, we'd find our way to the St. Nicholas Arena to watch such lightweight stalwarts as Havana, Cuba's Orlando Zulueta (great name), Toronto, Canada's Arthur King (very underrated), and other warriors in action. (I think a ticket costs two dollars.)

One night my all-time favorite baseball player Richie Ashburn, then playing with the New York Mets, was at St. Nick's seated a few rows in front of us, and I still regret not asking him for his autograph.

Another time, heavyweight contender Roland LaStarza was in the audience and gave us a friendly wave as we walked to our seats. And there was the time Oscar winner Ed Begley, so outstanding in 1956's *Patterns*, was introduced and the crowd responded with loud applause. My point: You never really knew who was in the audience at either St. Nicholas Arena.

3

Kerouac concludes his piece on Parker by saying that "Dan Parker was the dean of American sportswriters because he wrote a long column every night, using dialects which were Italian, Jewish, Greek, French-Canadian, Irish, Polish. . . . After Dan Parker there can be no other sportswriter in America."

Any arguments?

A WINTER SPORTS STORY

1

So you want a winter sports story, right? You got it.

Let's go back to the mid-1960s, to New York City and the old Madison Square Garden. A friend and I traveled to the Big Apple by train from New Haven and paid ten dollars for some very good seats to see a Saturday afternoon game between New York Rangers and the Chicago Black Hawks. If you're a Blueshirts' fan, I'm certain you recall the mid-'60s were the Andy Bathgate and Lou Fontinato years. (Any Andy B. and Leapin' Looie fans out there?)

By the way today there are thirty-two NHL teams, but in the 1960s, there were six: Boston, New York, Chicago, Detroit, Toronto, and Montreal.

I don't remember the score of that Chicago-New York game, but in the third period the Hawks' Bobby Hull scored the most exciting goal I ever saw, and, lads and lassies, I've been watching hockey for a long time. In football what Hull did would've been tantamount to a 120-yard touchdown. You see, he skated the entire length of the Garden ice to score. He flew by the Rangers' players. There was no stopping number nine. After Hull scored even hardcore New York fans gave him a standing ovation.

2

Here's a more recent hockey story that took place on November 26, 2021. At 10:00 a.m., four friends and I took off for Boston's TD Garden to see the Boston Bruins battle the Rangers in an afternoon game. When we arrived, we met my son who had taken the train from New Hampshire to Boston.

Fifty-yard line seats. Eight rows up from the ice. And the Rangers won, 5-2. But what made my day wasn't only the Blueshirts' victory but the reception I received before the game.

Reception? I'll explain.

I decided before we left Connecticut that morning for Boston to wear my Hartford Whalers jersey. That's right! The non-existent Hartford Whalers who when they did exist in the NHL—which was from 1979 to 1997— were Boston's bitter rivals.

After we arrived at the TD Garden, much to my delight at least seven fans gave me thumbs up when they saw the jersey. On the escalator leading into the Garden one young guy pointed at me, paused, and said, "Hey! Nice jersey."

After we took our seats, I told one of my friends I was surprised and delighted by the reception I had received. Without pausing he brazenly replied, "They weren't giving you a thumbs up. What's wrong with you? They were giving you the middle finger." And he laughed.

And he's probably still laughing.

That those Boston fans were giving me the finger is BULLSHIT! They were thumbs upping me because, thank you very much, they recognized a class act when they saw one.

ABOUT THE AUTHOR

Somehow Roger Zotti, who was born in New Haven, Connecticut, graduated from high school. His first attempt at college was a failure, but several years later he tried again, this time at Eastern Connecticut State College, and did quite well, to the amazement of himself and everyone who knew him.

After graduating from Eastern, he went on to earn a master's degree in literature from Wesleyan University in 1971, and then to teach adult education at a Connecticut Correctional Center for over twenty years, retiring in 1993.

He has many interests: The WNBA Connecticut Sun, old and new movies, music, hockey — specifically, the Hartford Wolfpack, New York Rangers, and, yes, the non-existent Hartford Whalers — reading, running, writing, and collecting Scripto lead pencils (especially the red ones).

He and his wife live in Preston, Connecticut, along with Remi, their mischievous and creative dog. They have two adult children, Tom and Leslie.

Currently, he's a regular contributor to the *International Boxing Research Journal* and a member of its editorial board. Also, he serves on the Connecticut Boxing Hall of Fame Induction committee.

One of his several philosophies of life is, to quote Mel Brooks, "nothing helps you to succeed like failure."

He can be reached at rogerzotti@aol.com. But contact him only if you're going to praise his writing!